HIS FIRE AND HIS ICE

HIS FIRE AND HIS ICE

SHAMEKA S ERBY

Contents

Copyright

Dedication

To the ones who think they're not enough...

You are. And then some.

Content Warning

Gunplay, violence, death, mentions of parental death and illegal
activities

Author's Note

This is a poly-amorous, closed triad, romance. There are explicit sex scenes on page, and mentions of impact play.

Prologue

One Year Ago
<u>*Romelo*</u>

"Romelo! Is she here?! Are you hiding her?" Sadie Marie Wells screamed as she walked through the house and into Romelo "King" Davis's office. Her steps were hard, and her face flushed with anger and hurt. Romelo could see her coming down the hall toward him, her big titties heaving with exertion, braids swinging, wide hips switching, her plushness bouncing all over as she waved a piece of paper in her hand. Her cute little upturned rose was red against her light brown skin, and he could tell she'd been crying. Still, his girlfriend's girlfriend was gorgeous. If Bianca had anything, it was impeccable taste in women. Scratch and Teddy, Romelo's guards, followed behind her, rolling their eyes at her tirade. He'd told them to expect her.

"Sadie, come sit down. Why don't you—"

"No. NO. I want to know if she's here. Is she under the damn desk sucking your dick, afraid to face me? Is that why you're so calm, Romelo?"

"Of course not. Sadie—"

"Get your ass out here, Bianca Bellamy! What, did she pick you and not want to tell me? Did you convince her she didn't need me? BIANCA!!!"

"Gotdammit, Sadie, stop yelling. If you let me speak—" he started, his ears ringing from her screaming, but Sadie slapped the letter down on the desk, turning to look out into the hallway where even Scratch and Teddy were now cowering in the face of her anger.

"Fuck this! You'd better tell her to come out here and break up with me like a grown fucking woman. I deserve better. If she—"

"Sadie!" Romelo barked, finally interrupting her. He sighed deeply and slid an identical letter onto the desk, looking right into her red-rimmed eyes. "She's not here. She left me too."

Sadie swallowed, her words running out as she stared at him. She sank into a chair in front of his desk, and he went around to her, sitting in the one beside her and taking her hand.

"She's gone? She...you too?" she whispered, her breaths speeding up. Sadie closed her eyes, letting two tears fall. Her hands shook and her body slumped, as if her anger had tired her.

"I got in from a meeting a couple of hours ago. The letter was waiting for me when I got back. I haven't seen her since she left to spend the night with you yesterday. She must have come in sometime today and left it." Romelo spoke softly, rubbing Sadie's palm with his thumb. Knowing their girlfriend really was gone, she was visibly distressed and seemed lost. He couldn't deny he wasn't feeling much better.

Romelo met Bianca Bellamy two years before, and he fell in love immediately. His heart connecting fast was a family trait; his cousin Trevino had known his man Bashir would take his heart the day he met him. Romelo had no qualms about laying his heart bare to Bianca. He just worried she wouldn't return the favor. After all, she was a dancer who wanted her name in lights, and he was a drug kingpin and weapons trafficker. But Bianca fell in love with him too. She told him she was polyamorous, and he was fine in an open relationship. His side was closed; he'd wanted only her, but he wasn't a jealous or selfish man. Romelo knew what he brought to the table. There were whispers about him losing respect among his team for "letting his woman play him with that sharing shit," but the King caught the whisperers and responded out loud with fury and gasoline, watching calmly as they danced to death in the flames. There were no more whispers after.

Six months into their relationship, Bianca introduced him to Sadie Wells—a vibrant, hot-tempered, stubborn, spoiled she-devil who loved guns and wouldn't hesitate to use one. The fire to Bianca's ice. She assured him he and Sadie were all she wanted in the world, and it was all the motivation *they* needed to make their three-way relationship as harmonious as possible. They'd become friends, collaborating on gifts and celebrations for their number one girl. Romelo thought they were all happy. But now Bianca was gone, like a thief in the night, leaving nothing but two letters to explain why she'd broken two hearts.

I guess we weren't all happy.

"I don't understand why she would do this," Sadie said, her voice a tearful mumble. Romelo kept rubbing her palm, hoping to soothe her and himself.

"My guess is she wanted a clean break," he replied. "With her auditioning for the lead with this new dance troupe, she probably thought she'd be on the road so much our relationships would suffer. She ended them now to save us all some heartbreak later."

Sadie sucked her teeth. "She ended them because she's a damn scaredy cat. Yes, things would have changed, been more challenging, but I knew what Bee did when I met her. I wasn't going anywhere."

"Neither was I. But it doesn't matter what we knew. It matters what she believed. And she believed she was doing the right thing."

"How the fuck are you so calm about this?" Sadie demanded. Romelo chuckled, rolling his shoulders to release the tension.

"There's some shot-up targets in my gun range out back that would suggest I'm not calm at all," he answered. Sadie giggled, pulling her hands from his to wipe her face.

"Can we go out there? I need to shoot something too."

Romelo stood up, reaching for Sadie's hand again. He pulled her from the chair and into his arms quickly, kissing the top of her head. They'd had their hearts broken by the same woman. As strange a bond as it was, they were bonded. He'd take care of Sadie. Romelo had a feeling it was what Bianca would want.

"Of course. Let's go," he said, and he and Sadie headed to the shooting range behind his house.

Three Months Later

Sadie

"Romelo! I brought lunch!" Sadie yelled as she headed to his office. Scratch and Teddy shook their heads; they were used to her loudness by now. She opened the office door and went in, setting the bag with their lunch on the desk and sitting down. Romelo was talking on one cell phone while he texted on another, a hollowed-out book filled with small bags of white powder and stacks of money open in front of him. He smiled at her, and his brown eyes lit up.

Romelo "King" Davis was easily the finest man she'd ever seen in her life. His skin was the color of sandstone, brown and orange hues mixing deliciously in a perfect swirl, setting off his chubby cheeks and toffee eyes. He had a wide nose, slightly crooked from a teenage break not healing correctly, and thick, curved lips that were positively sinful. Romelo was huge—six foot two and wide-bodied, bulked by muscles and fat in equal measure. His chest was hard, but his belly was soft, and she loved sinking into him whenever he hugged her.

"You got 'til Tuesday. And because you feel like you can play with me, Truck will be there to collect. Yeah, yeah, whatever." Romelo put both phones down and closed the hollowed-out book. With Sadie there every day, he no longer worried about what she saw—he knew she'd keep it to herself. Sadie started unpacking food after he wiped the desktop and his hands. He dug into the steak sandwich she brought him, taking two huge bites and grunting as he ate.

She watched him eat, suddenly noticing the thickness of his lips as he wrapped them around the sandwich, the sharpness of his white teeth sinking into the bread, steak, cheese, and onions, his strong jaw moving as he chewed, his toffee eyes closing in relief as he eased his hunger. Sadie noticed everything today, and it was like she'd never seen any of it before. Today, it was different. Today, it was...affecting her.

"What's the point of you having someone here to cook if you skip meals?" Sadie questioned, trying to regulate her thoughts as she took a much more delicate bite of her own sandwich. Romelo swallowed his food and rolled his eyes.

"Woman, what I tell you about lecturing me when I'm eating?"

"Somebody has to. You need to take better care of yourself. You're working to keep yourself distracted and busy and you're wasting away. I don't like it."

"Your grumpy ass doesn't like anything," he mumbled, taking another bite. Sadie opened her mouth to deny, then shut it when she realized she couldn't. Romelo was exhausted and mired in work, and she was crabby and ill-tempered, irritated by everything, especially happy things.

In the three months Bianca had been gone, she and Romelo had grown closer, leaning on each other as friends and confidants, their connection cemented over late-night drinking sessions, movie nights in his theater room, and hours spent out back, shooting targets to vent their anger.

At first, Sadie begged him to track Bee down. She knew with Romelo's considerable resources it was very possible for him to find out where she'd gone. But he denied her, saying if Bianca wanted space, they should give it to her, and they deserved better than having to chase after her. Sadie didn't want to agree but had to concede he was right. Bianca had to learn the hard way no one would love her better than them, and Sadie knew the lesson was coming. But in the meantime, Romelo pushed deeper into work, and she snapped at everyone...for everything.

"I'm going out back after we finish," she announced. "I want to shoot something."

"Not today," Romelo refused, swallowing his last bite. "I can't take the noise. My head is killing me."

Sadie pouted; Romelo never denied her anything. But she didn't protest. It was his house, after all. And if his head was hurting, his rest was more important since his migraines had joined his eating and sleeping habits as another thing that was getting worse.

They sat in the office for a few more minutes, then Romelo took a bottle of water from the mini fridge beside him and said he was going up to his room. She had free rein in his house, and everything was alarmed and guarded, so he had no issue leaving her alone. He knew she was safe. Sadie thought about going home, but she didn't want to be alone. She decided she would hole up in Romelo's theater room and watch movies and implement her usual plan of bugging Scratch and Teddy until one of them watched with her.

Halfway into the movie, Sadie decided to check on Romelo. She hopped up, heading to the second level and knocking on the French doors that opened to his primary suite. There was no answer, and Sadie tried the door, finding it unlocked. She ducked in, shutting the door behind her, and walked quietly through his sitting room into the bedroom area. Romelo was in bed, the room dark and quiet to help relieve the pain in his head. She could see his eyes were closed, but his breathing was so stuttered and choppy she knew he wasn't sleeping.

"Melo?" Sadie called him softly. Romelo opened his eyes, staring at her. He sat up and lifted his hand, gesturing towards her. As if he'd given her feet permission to move, Sadie hurried to the side of the bed, kicking off her sneakers and climbing in. He immediately pulled her on top of him, holding her so tight she could barely breathe.

"Is this, okay?" he whispered.

Sadie nodded into his chest. It was better than okay. His body was warm and hard against her softness. It'd been so long since someone held her, relief and pure instinct made her snuggle closer. Romelo growled deep in his throat, pleased with her touch. Sadie breathed in his scent, closing her own eyes. The two of them were closer these days, and very affectionate, but this felt different. It felt like sweetness and desire, like warm honey and slow kisses. It felt like something not about Bianca at all.

"Is your head better?" she asked, keeping her voice soft. Romelo rubbed slow circles on her back, the pressure of his hands more comforting than a weighted blanket.

"Nah, not really," he answered her. Sadie sat up, looking into his eyes. She saw the same unsure desire she was feeling, along with pain from his headache. She lifted her hands to either side of his head, using her fingers to massage his temples. He sighed, gripping her hips as she straddled him. His eyes drifted closed and his face relaxed. Sadie smiled. Next time, she'd bring some lavender oil to soothe him even more. She continued her massage, humming in a soft voice while Romelo rubbed her hips and thighs. Sadie felt her desire increasing, making her want to grind on his lap and create more friction against his dick, which was slowly hardening underneath her. But she forced herself to focus. Romelo was hurting, and he needed her.

"Your hands feel so good, Shug," Romelo whispered into the quiet. Sadie blinked, momentarily confused. He'd never called her anything but her name before. Her body warmed with affection at the thought of getting her own nickname. He'd always called

Bianca "Baby Girl." She pushed away thoughts of their ex and refocused on making Romelo feel better. He was squeezing her ass now, lifting his hips so she could feel that he was fully hard.

Sadie gulped. She and Romelo were friends. They leaned on each other, took care of each other. They were healing together. Desiring more seemed greedy, given how their closeness started. But she wanted Romelo, and it seemed he wanted her too. Neither of them had any idea what was happening, but there was no way Sadie would be the one to stop it. She leaned forward, kissing him before she could talk herself out of it. He only hesitated a second before kissing her back, his lips firm and warm on hers. They moaned at the same time.

Lips pressed and tasted, and soon their tongues were in the game. Sadie's hands fell from Romelo's head to his shoulders, and she gripped him tightly, pleasure blooming from the crown of her head to the soles of her feet. Kissing Romelo felt like something she'd been waiting her entire life to do. Their mouths made love and Sadie whimpered, eager for more. Romelo's tongue was thick and wrapped around hers, pulling them both deeper into the swarm of their desire. His hands were busy, caressing her curves, gripping her body, palming her softness.

Sadie was burning up now, and she wanted his skin against hers. She sat back, pulling her top over her head. Her pink lace bra was a simple scrap, barely holding her large breasts, and Romelo smiled as he stared at her hard nipples. He reached up and grabbed the bra in the middle, ripping it open. Sadie gasped in surprise and then pleasure as his mouth covered her breast. He suckled her, hard, and she moaned. She arched her back, pushing her breast further into his hot mouth. Romelo's fingers pulled at her other nipple, prepping it for its turn between his lips.

"Dammit, Melo," Sadie protested weakly, "fucking bra costs me fifty bucks."

"Then it's a good thing I ripped that cheap shit," he replied, his mouth still against her. He licked her between his words, making her dig her nails into his shoulders. "You getting in this bed means you mine now, and when you mine, everything touching your body should reflect that you got a nigga with *infinite* pockets. You hearing me, Sadie Marie?"

His arrogant edict, the growl of her full name, and his tongue on her nipple sent Sadie into orbit, and she nodded, too aroused to form words. Romelo pulled back, staring into her eyes. His were dark and stormy, filled with desire and something else she wouldn't dare name out loud.

"No nodding. I need to know you with me. Do you understand, Shug?" he whispered, reverting to her new nickname, and Sadie swallowed. He tugged on her nipples as he spoke and she wet her panties, her breathing harsh and choppy. She heard the urgency in his voice, the desperation...the anxiety. He needed to know he wasn't in this alone.

"I understand," she whispered back.

"Understand what?" he demanded. Sadie licked her lips, moved in his lap, felt his hard dick. She couldn't wait to have it inside of her.

"I'm yours, and everything touching me should reflect it."

"Good girl," Romelo praised her and went back to sucking and licking on her. Sadie moaned his name, her senses overloaded with pleasure and new love. She understood Romelo was offering his heart and body and she wanted both with a fierceness she'd never expected. He pushed her to the side and underneath him, flipping their positions so he was on top. His mouth released her breast, Sadie's whimper of protest swallowed when he kissed her again. Their lips and tongues tangled, and her hands went around Romelo's neck, running her fingers over his nape, eliciting groans from him.

"Shug, I need you bad. Can I have you?" Romelo whispered against her lips. Sadie nipped at his mouth, licked his sexy smile.

"Of course, you can, baby. I'm yours, remember?" she whispered back. Romelo grinned, leaning up to tug off her pants and underwear. Seconds later, her big thighs were spread wide, and he was buried deep, catching them both off guard with how good it felt. Sadie came almost immediately, her body on edge, her senses dancing. Romelo sank into her wet pussy like it was home, and as far as either of them were concerned, now it was.

Sadie held him to her, moaning at his deep thrusts. She heard what he hadn't said. The invitation to his bed was his declaration that he was hers to have. Hers to keep. Hers to love. He'd needed to know she felt the same. And she did. Romelo Davis had healed her heart. It was only right it become his now.

And nine months later... Bianca is the next to come home. But is there still room for her?

One

<u>*ianca*</u>

B Bianca Bellamy sighed, leaning into the hard chest pressed against her back. The man laying behind her in bed grabbed her thigh, lifting her leg and sliding his hard dick inside her. She moaned softly, loving the intrusion, the fullness. She was desperate to be filled; she felt so empty sometimes.

"My God, you are beautiful," the man whispered in her ear. Bianca closed her eyes, tuning out his voice. She didn't need him to tell her. If there was one thing she already knew, it was that. She needed him to fill her, over and over, until she forgot her heart was a desolate wasteland of her own making. Until she forgot she pushed away the man and woman who used to occupy it. The man thrust deeply, moving his hips in time with hers, caressing the underside of her leg where he held it up for easier access. Bianca sighed again, feeling the delicious pleasure of his dick and the build of what she knew would be a wonderful orgasm.

"As good as you two look, I'm not going to be left out," the woman said, moving closer and leaning down to close her lips around Bianca's hard nipple. Bianca whimpered, the sensations giving her goosebumps. She'd been fucking this married couple for a few months, and every encounter was better than the last. Every session in their bed relaxed her mind, flooded her body with endorphins, and temporarily blocked the guilt in her heart. Every session made her forget how carelessly she threw away the only two people who mattered to her. Every session took her to the heights of her delicious, sexual, fantasies and made her feel a little foolish for being too afraid to ask Romelo and Sadie to fuck her at the same time. The three of them together would have been explosive.

The woman sucked harder, swirling her tongue around Bianca's nipple and caressing her smooth stomach. Bianca moaned, loving the feel of her body being wielded by others for their pleasure and hers. The bedroom was the only place she felt comfortable giving up control, and she'd been blessed to find Tanya and Charlie—a mature, sophisticated couple who took her emotional distance in stride, respected her space when she wasn't in their bed, and played with her body like their favorite toy whenever she was.

"More," Bianca begged as Tanya reached down to strum her clit and Charlie fucked her harder. She heard his grunts in her ear, felt his chest dampen with sweat, and his heart pound. Tanya whimpered as she watched her husband's dick get slick with Bianca's cum and Bianca knew Tanya would cum as well; watching was her favorite thing to do. Charlie's dick was an impressive size, and his sexual appetite was huge; he reminded Bianca of Romelo in that way.

"Kiss me," Bianca demanded, opening her eyes to look at Tanya. Tanya grinned and leaned up, touching their lips and tongues together. The two women moaned into each other's mouths. Bianca grabbed Tanya's breast, tugged on her nipple, and rolled it between her fingers. Tanya was a curvy woman, her body round and soft, and the feel of her reminded Bianca so much of her beloved Sadie she often had to stop herself from saying her ex's name. The differences between her and Tanya's bodies was another thing she loved. While Tanya was all plush and jiggly, with fat cheeks on her face and ass, Bianca was leggy, slim faced with a tight ass, and slender, her genetics simply keeping her hips wide, her breasts sizable, and the smallest jiggle in her belly.

Charlie thrust hard, groaning. He was close to finishing, and Bianca moved her hips, wanting to finish with him. Tanya's fingers now moved swiftly between her own thighs, circling her clit over and over as she and Bianca shared, wet, lush, kisses. Bianca slapped Tanya's hands away and took over, rubbing the woman's swollen, wet, clit with force—the way she liked it.

"Bee!" Tanya yelled out, wrenching her mouth away. She shook and her back arched, her orgasm crashing over her. Charlie bit down on Bianca's shoulder, his pelvis slapping against her ass as he started to cum, grunting his pleasure. Their mutual climax tipped her own, and Bianca fell off the cliff, gasping for breath and shaking. The three of them were moaning and grabbing for each other, ending up a tangled pile of limbs and satisfaction. Bianca smiled. She needed to get up, shower, and dodge Tanya's attempts to get her to spend the night, but for a moment, she was blissed out and completely sated.

"Are you sure you don't want to stay?' Tanya asked, feeding Bianca her Italian hoagie. Bianca took a bite of the sandwich, wondering why they needed to go through this every time. She never spent the night. It was bad enough she still felt like she was fucking around on Romelo and Sadie; the least she could do was not wake up next to other people. Bianca chewed, trying to think of yet another way to speak her mind without hurting Tanya's feelings. Tanya was kind, beautiful, and funny. Plus, her pussy was good, and she knew how to use her hands and mouth. Bianca couldn't piss her off. She couldn't lose her too. Losing Sadie was hard enough.

"Tan, leave her alone. Bee needs her space. We've gotta respect it," Charlie said, coming to sit down at the table with them, his big hands wrapped around a sandwich. Bianca sighed in relief. Charlie understood. He supported her choice and gave her the space to sort out her own shit. He really was like Romelo. She turned to him, smiling widely.

"Thank you, baby. I'm easing into this as much as I can. But I have to go at my own pace. You guys understand, right?"

"Of course we do," Charlie said, taking a huge bite of his sandwich, "Our door will stay open for whenever you're ready to walk through."

"And your room is ready," Tanya said, smiling as she fed Bianca more sandwich. Bianca took another bite, her guilt lessening. She knew what she gave them wasn't nearly up to par with what they gave her, but she needed their affection and understanding so badly. It was the only thing making the nights bearable.

"You make the best subs, Tan," she praised, knowing the compliment would distract the other woman. After watching her husband fuck someone's brains out, Tanya's second love was feeding people. Preferably the people drained and satiated by her husband's dick. As Bianca thought, Tanya smiled even brighter.

"I'm glad you're enjoying it, Buttercup. I'll make one you can have for a late-night snack when you get home. You know you get hungry in the middle of the night."

"It sounds good, but I don't want to feel heavy when I get to rehearsals. I'll ignore the craving and eat it for lunch tomorrow."

"Don't ignore your hunger, Buttercup. It's not good for you," Tanya insisted. Bianca smiled. This woman was so damn sweet.

"Bee is grown, Tan. I'm sure she can manage her own appetite," Charlie jumped in.

Tanya pouted. "I know she can. But I can still be concerned."

"Of course you can, baby. And I appreciate it," Bianca said, leaning forward for a kiss. Tanya's lips met hers and they both sighed, pressing their mouths together. Affection, sex, care, and concern. But still freedom, autonomy, support, and encouragement. These two were amazing. It was almost like being with Romelo and Sadie again. Almost.

Later that night, Bianca wrapped her thighs around her favorite body pillow and hugged it close. Contrary to what she led Tanya and Charlie to believe, she hated sleeping alone. But she refused to get comfortable in their home, refused to settle into their life, refused to dishonor her heart more than she already had by getting involved with them. Tanya and Charlie Nance were a great addition to her life after what happened. But Romelo Davis and Sadie Wells were her heart's desire. There was no changing it, and she didn't want to.

The next day there was a flurry of rehearsals and costume adjustments. There was a show later that night, and everyone was rushing around trying to make sure things were perfect. Bianca spent her time as she usually did, in one of the small empty studios' backstage, alone in her own world, stretching and readying her body. She was friendly with the rest of the troupe, but not close, and maybe it was better that way. Tanya and Charlie weren't anyone's business, and the only other thing she had to talk about was how much she missed what she left behind.

Bianca was a lead dancer with a well-known hip-hop ballet dance troupe, and they were currently touring the West Coast. The day she left Romelo and Sadie was the day she found out the troupe wanted her as a principal dancer. The director and choreographer both raved over her audition piece, and said it was innovative and technically flawless. It was a dream come true, and she'd been ecstatic and scared. Traveling all over the country was no life for a woman committed to two people. She wouldn't be home enough, and everything would suffer. And even if they could come to where she was, what time would she have to spend with them, if she was focused on shows and learning new routines? It seemed easier to break things off. Bianca knew it was wrong to leave the way she had, but she wasn't brave enough to break Romelo and Sadie's hearts to their faces. She always hoped the letters she wrote assured them she loved them both so completely, and it wasn't anything they'd done.

"Bianca! Ro got sick—we need you for the second sequence!" the assistant choreographer yelled, walking over and interrupting Bianca's musings. It was just as well. Thoughts of her loves always made her a little sad, and Show Day was no day to let her emotions come through her dancing. This was a high energy performance.

"Who's going to take my place in the third?" she asked, rising to her feet. The assistant choreographer, a perpetually cheerful guy named Seven, shrugged.

"We'll get Lana to understudy you in the third. We're asking you because we know you usually memorize the whole show and will pick up a lot quicker than someone else. You good?"

"Yeah, Sev, I'm good. Should I start going over the second sequence or make sure Lana has the third down?"

"Don't worry about Lana. You find T.C. so he can walk you through the second sequence. I'm pretty sure you've got it, but we want you to be ready," Seven replied and walked away, heading to deliver more assignments and yell at people to tighten up. Bianca headed to the stage area, knowing it was where T.C. was posted up. As a principal male dancer, and everyone's surrogate big brother, he liked to see everything coming together. It was never about any one individual performance with T.C. It was always about the whole. He was a big picture man; it was why people loved him.

"T.C.!" Bianca called to him as she approached the side of the stage where he was watching, "Sev told me I should see you about the second sequence choreo. I think I've got it down, but we can still run through it."

T.C. Norris turned to her, a smile on his handsome face. He was medium brown, doe-eyed, thick-lipped, and gorgeous. He had those wonderfully thick lashes women would kill for and locs down his back. He was a shameless flirt, and aware of how fine he was, but no one took him seriously, because he was madly in love, and had a partner who didn't play about him.

"I was hoping Seven would ask you, Bee Baby. You pay attention to the work, and you move so effortlessly," T.C. said, winking at her as she stopped in front of him.

Bianca smirked. "You're just saying that because I have the routine memorized. Less work for you."

"Hell yeah. Come on, let's run it down a couple times, make sure our timing and positioning are good," he said back. Bianca got on her mark, facing T.C. and the two of them began to dance in their small corner of the huge stage. Others stopped to watch, but the two of them were only concerned with getting it perfect for the performance. After the second run through, there was scattered applause and T.C. soaked it up, waving and blowing kisses, like he was the mayor on a parade float. Seven broke up the moment, yelling at everyone to get back to work while Bianca giggled. The troupe was a good time, and she loved the energy, even if she wasn't the most personable.

"I heard... you turned down a Golden Ticket," T.C. said as the two of them wiped down with towels and went in search of water. Bianca stared at him. Was nothing a secret around here?

"It wasn't my Golden Ticket. It was an... opportunity. And it wasn't for me," she replied, hoping her tone would halt any further questions.

In her industry, a "Golden Ticket" was slang for an unbeatable opportunity. For some dancers, it was the chance to do something impactful and creative, in an environment closer to home, with minimal travel. Bianca had been offered first consideration for a principal dancer and artist-in-residence position with a newly formed ballet company based in her hometown. The place she'd run away from. The place where she'd left Romelo and Sadie.

"You sure, Bee baby? I would have thought it was right up your alley. I know how hard it was for you to leave your people."

"It was fine. I'm fine—th-they understood. I-I mean, they understand," Bianca tried to recover. T.C. smirked, clearly not believing her. He sucked down half a bottle of water, staring at her while she tried to avoid his eyes. When he finally pulled the bottle from his mouth, he shook his head.

"I see now. You're running," he said.

"Excuse me?"

"You didn't leave home, you ran away. And you don't want to deal with whatever chaos you left in your wake, so you don't want to go back."

"That's —it is not—"

"Come on, Bianca. Keep it real with me. You were offered something amazing, something that would put you right where you want to be, and won't derail your career, and you won't even consider it? There's gotta be a reason other than, 'it wasn't for me.'"

"Okay, yes. I ran away from something. It's complicated, and I don't do complicated. What else do you want me to say to you, T.C?"

"I don't want you to say shit to me, but the tone of your voice suggests there's someone else you need to say something to," T.C. said, side eyeing her as put down his water bottle and started stretching. Bianca turned away, embarrassed, and ashamed. He was right. There were so many words unsaid between her, Romelo, and Sadie, and she was too cowardly to even attempt to reach out. She'd carelessly thrown her two hearts away; acting like a petulant child wouldn't get them back. Bianca started her own stretches, taking deep breaths and pushing her arms out to her sides.

"I'm sorry, T.C. You're right. I do need to speak to them, but it's too late. The way I left was... I'm sure they hate me," Bianca said, sighing. T.C. lifted his leg and held it over his head in a standing split, watching her.

"Them?" he finally asked.

Bianca nodded, dropping into a plié. "I had two partners, a man and a woman. I loved them both, but this job came up and I got scared I wouldn't be able to maintain things with them. I thought it'd be easier to leave, let them both start fresh. I miss them every day, and I—I know I need to apologize, but it freaks me out to even think about trying to."

"Then you have to do it," T.C. declared. Bianca stared at him, mouth agape.

"Wh—what?" she demanded.

T.C. shrugged. "We don't let you hide with the company. We make you face fear. Whatever move you're scared to try, lift you're scared to attempt, piece you think is too complicated, it's the exact thing Sev makes you do. Folks think he's some kind of punisher, but he simply pays attention. He figures out your fear, and makes you confront it. Going home got you shaking in your pointe shoes, so of course it's exactly what you have to do."

"But what if I see them? What do I say to them?"

"Depends on what you want from them. Do you want them back?"

"No I—it's too la—they'd never—"

"Bianca," T.C. grabbed her hand and looked into her eyes, "do you want them back?"

Bianca felt tears coming to her eyes. This past year without Romelo and Sadie had been a haze of pain and loneliness. She loved her job and was able to empty her mind and pretend as she danced in show after show, but she missed them. She missed Sadie's smart mouth, her soft body, and her trigger-happy personality; she missed Romelo's silent strength, his insatiable appetite for her and food, and his sexy, smoldering demeanor. Bianca needed her lovers. She wanted to go home.

"Yes," she mumbled, turning away to wipe the tears on her face, "I want them back."

"Then take the Golden Ticket and go home, Bee. It's been a year, and your heart is still with them. You gotta try."

"What if they don't want me?" Bianca whispered, her body going cold at the thought. T.C. gave her a sad smile.

"The Bianca Bellamy I know ain't never stopped at the first rejection. How many times did you audition for this company before you got in?"

"Three," she admitted, smiling a little herself.

T.C. chuckled. "Exactly. You take notes, you tighten up, and you come back harder. If you still love them, you gotta go home and tell them."

Bianca sniffled a little, nodding. T.C. was right. She'd run away like a child, and she was getting a perfect opportunity to fix things, like an adult. She couldn't turn away. It was time to go home. Bianca only hoped Romelo and Sadie would be willing to listen and let her convince them she was home to stay.

Romelo and Sadie

"Shug, I don't know why your spoiled ass thinks you can interrupt my meetings any time you want."

"Because I can. Those niggas will never be more important than me."

"Of course not. But I still have a business to run. Now what the hell is so urgent?"

"I think something's happening down on 46th," Sadie Wells told her man as he sat in the chair at his desk and she sat on his desk, right in front of him.

Romelo Davis smirked. "And why do you think so?"

"Because I've replaced three burner phones in a month for their crew. I don't mind, but I think it's strange," she replied. Sadie was Romelo's Equipment Specialist. She managed their personal armory of weapons and communication devices.

"Three, huh?" Romelo said, rubbing her thigh with one hand while he twirled a pen between his fingers with the other hand.

"Yes! You need to do a pop-up and see what's going on. You can't sit up in the ivory tower while shit is happening in the streets. You have to remind these niggas you're still on the pulse of everything," Sadie insisted. Romelo grinned. He loved it when Shug got worked up like this. He hated when she interrupted his meetings to do it, but he loved how she constantly looked out for his interests.

Romelo put his pen down and palmed both of Sadie's thighs, rubbing them as he leaned forward. She leaned down and the two of them kissed, sweetly at first, then more hungrily. Sadie moaned and Romelo slid his chair up and settled between his woman's legs, his hands moving over her stockings and up underneath her dress. He felt Sadie's smooth skin where the stockings stopped and felt the fastening of her garter belt.

"Melo, I didn't mean to interrupt, but I needed you," Sadie whispered. Romelo kept kissing her, tasting her lips, sucking her tongue into his mouth. Meanwhile, his hands kept rubbing higher, heading for the warmth he could feel at the apex of her wonderful thighs. Sadie had removed her panties for his easy access, sure she'd be successful in distracting him and Romelo took advantage, cupping her warm pussy. His thumb slipped between her pussy lips, finding her clit and circling it.

"Ooh baby," Sadie whimpered, opening her legs wider. Romelo kissed her silent, rubbing her clit harder and faster, catching every sound in his own mouth. Sadie was drowning in pleasure, moving her hips in time with his hand, running her nails up and down Romelo's neck and shoulders. His tongue tasted like the coffee he'd drank and the donut he consumed with it and Sadie licked at him, loving his delicious, sugary kisses. This man was so sexy he made her ache.

Romelo finally lifted his lips from hers and Sadie took a gasping breath, throwing her head back as soft cries pushed out of her throat. His thumb moved faster, pressed harder.

"Bet you ready to come, huh, Shug?" he whispered. Sadie nodded, riding a wave of rapture. The crash was going to be magnificent. One stroke, two, three. Another and she'd be over the cliff. Sadie gasped, ready—

"Wait, what?" she opened her eyes, breathless and confused as Romelo pulled his hand from between her thighs. He licked his fingers, savoring her juices while he grinned at her.

"Oh, you weren't done?" he shrugged innocently, leaning back in his chair. Sadie's eyes widened. *I know this bastard ain't about to leave me hanging*, she thought.

"No, I wasn't done, Romelo! And you know I wasn't! Why did you stop? I was right there, and then you—"

"Interrupted?" He finished her sentence, his smile turning sinister, "Kinda like you did to me in my meeting. I was ready to wrap up a deal, and you... interrupted."

"Romelo I—"

"Aht aht," he held up his hand, stopping her, "When my needs get cut short, yours will too. I told you about that shit, Sadie."

"This is not fair. You got out of bed before the sun was up, we didn't make love this morning, and I haven't seen you all day! I needed you, Romelo."

"So, you walk into my meeting with your dress barely covering your thighs and no damn panties on to lie to me about an emergency? You know better," Romelo shot back, glaring at her.

Sadie scowled. She knew she was acting spoiled and on Romelo's last nerves as usual, but she missed him whenever he was out of her sight, and she wasn't sure how to process it. Keona coming home to be with Easy, right after Nasima came home to be with Trevino and Bashir, made her feel like she and Romelo were lacking their usual closeness. Everyone around her was in the honeymoon phase, and it felt like she and Romelo had been relegated to the old married couple of the group.

"I do, and I'm sorry. But you told me to pull your card when you weren't making us a priority. You said I could call you out when you weren't keeping your word. We're supposed to be the most important thing," Sadie explained herself as best she could and Romelo's eyes softened.

"I know, and we are, baby. But you could have caught me after the meeting and talked to me. Instead, you barge in when I'm talking to niggas I gotta trust with my money and product, making me look like I can't even run my own household," Romelo explained himself.

Sadie shook her head. "I didn't mean to undermine you, baby. I understand, and I'll do better."

"I'm sorry for making you feel unimportant, Shug. You're my reason, and my number one. Always," Romelo apologized and slid forward again. The two of them exchanged a passionate kiss and Romelo put his hands back where they were, giving Sadie the release and connection she'd been seeking when she first interrupted his meeting. Moments later, Sadie climaxed on a high pitch cry, and Romelo was happy he'd soundproofed his office. After she was calmer, Sadie hopped down from the desk and bent over it, her bare ass swaying in his face. Romelo stood up, opening his pants and pushing them down. Two seconds later, he was filling her, driving into her hard, nailing her to his desk with punishing strokes. He raised his hand, bringing it down on her ass cheek with a resounding smack. Sadie yelped, pushing back against him harder. She loved it when he took charge of her, when he bent her to his will. He spanked her again, making a red handprint on her light brown ass. Her pussy fluttered, tightening around him, and she got wetter.

"*Lo siento, Rey* (I'm sorry, King). I didn't mean it," she wailed. Sadie was fluent in Spanish and sometimes slipped into it in the heat of passion without noticing; in those moments she usually called him *Rey*, the Spanish translation of his street name, "King."

Romelo ignored her apology, fucked her harder, lost himself in her warm wetness. He spanked her a third time, and then again, until her whole ass was red.

"You better behave or I'm gonna stop making you cum," he said, his breath coming in short bursts, "You hear me?"

"Yes, baby. I'll be good, from now on. *Prometo* (I promise)," Sadie gasped. They both knew they were telling lies, but it heightened the urgency of their lovemaking, and they lived in the moment.

Romelo was immersed in Sadie's paradise, the center of her thighs holding the keys to his calm, and happiness. He loved this woman so much. It was impossible to quantify. And after Bianca, he'd thought it wouldn't happen. But Sadie Wells made her own place in his heart. She tried him every day, bugged and badgered him relentlessly and took as much of his attention for herself as she could. She was a giant pain in his ass and his heartbeat, all at once, and Romelo wouldn't change a thing.

He sped up, thrusting faster. Sadie was holding on for dear life, every push into her making her cry out. Her wetness coated the front of his thighs, and she was shaking, but she was still with him, fucking him back, taking him like she was made for it. She *was* made for it. For him.

"Romeloooooo," Sadie called his name, and her pussy tightened on him, squeezing as she dissolved into another orgasm. Romelo heard her cry, grunted in response and then groaned loudly as he came, pumping her full of his nut.

"I got you, Shug," he said, "I got you."

When they could move, they gathered themselves and went upstairs to their bedroom, where they freshened up and Romelo applied cool cloths to Sadie's behind, kissing her and soothing her reddened flesh. Then, they dressed again. Romelo had a late afternoon meeting, so there was no time for more debauchery. Sadie wore regular hosiery *and* underwear, since she was done trying to piss Romelo off.

"Oh, and I knew about 46th Street," Romelo said as they descended the stairs and headed into the den, where they held round-table meetings. Sadie smiled. She knew her man.

"Did you?"

"Yes, my baby. I sent Easy over there a couple of days ago to see what the deal was. As you can see, I do still have my finger on the pulse around here."

Sadie giggled. "I do see, lover. It's why you're the King. But what was going on?"

Romelo pulled out her chair and added a pillow in case she was still tender. Sadie smiled lovingly and he kissed her cheek as she sat down. "Turns out it was some domestic shit. One of Dave's new recruits, some little nigga with no home training, was cheating on his woman. She kept breaking the phones so he couldn't talk to other girls."

"Oh, my goodness," Sadie laughed, "What did Easy do?"

Easy and Truck walked in for the meeting. "I smacked Dave upside his fucking head for not noticing and then told the little nigga to tighten up. His name is Marco, or some shit. He got a crib and a kid with this girl. I told him his moves *in* his household reflect his character *outside*. He lets his old lady down, we know he ain't coming through for us. I asked him why *we* should trust him if his own family can't. Marco said he'd get his shit together, and Dave apologized for slipping. We'll see what happens next month."

"The melodrama," Sadie commented, still laughing. Romelo laughed as well and sat next to her. Truck and Easy sat down too and the four of them reviewed Sadie's information before their appointment showed up. Then she left the room, ducking into Romelo's office to watch from the camera feed streaming to the computer monitor. Scratch brought the two gentlemen into the room, and they took a seat.

Franco and Geraldo Acosta were brothers, in the small-time weapons business and trying to get bigger. They operated hours away, closer to where the Wolf's former compound was, which explained their visit.

The death of Kenyon Ross aka the Wolf, and the King's takeover of the Wolf's compound, had brought some other dealers in his area out of the woodwork, all wanting to know what would happen next. Was the King going to rebuild the Wolf's operations? Would they need to fight for the leftover territory? And if the Wolf died owing them, who was going to pay?

The last question was why the Acosta brothers had requested a meeting. They'd been in the middle of negotiating a weapons partnership with the Wolf when he met his demise. Since they knew Romelo wasn't willing to fill in as partner, they wanted him to sell them the Wolf's stockpile of weapons, which Romelo had no problem doing. He didn't need them, and paperwork they found in the Wolf's safe confirmed the weapons had been promised to the Acostas anyway.

"We don't want to take up too much of your time, King Davis. We need to get back home tonight," Franco said after pleasantries were exchanged.

"I understand. Our Equipment Specialist prepared a summary of the inventory we recovered and its estimated value," Romelo said, giving the brothers a small packet, detailing weapons by type and style, and the estimated value, given wear and use.

"We were under the impression the weapons were new," Geraldo said, reading the papers.

"Some of them were, but most were used, albeit only slightly. Kenyon had been living beyond his means for a while," Easy said, "He was hoping to have bartering tools for capital, and it didn't pan out. He was hemorrhaging funds badly." Easy's words had an edge of anger, but it was expected; his woman and son had been Kenyon's planned "bartering tools."

"There were plenty of guns that had simply been test fired. They were 'used,' but not really. We've marked those, and you can see they're at nearly full market value," Easy went on, showing the two brothers their system for categorizing. Franco and Geraldo nodded.

"We also need to talk professional courtesy and protocol," Truck leaned in, his hands on the table, "We know these weapons don't trace back to us—after all, we took them from a dead man—but we don't want them used in our name, or on our people. You start a war with somebody, and under pressure you admit we sold this shit back to you, then mufuckas start thinking we're orchestrating shit with Kenyon's enemies, and we not on that. All we wanted was him."

"Of course, we understand. As far as anyone knows, we partnered with Kenyon before he died, as planned," Franco said. Geraldo nodded.

"We not in y'all business, and we don't want to be. We got our own shit to handle. But don't get in ours... ever. And don't try to make us the middlemen," Easy said. Franco nodded again.

Romelo smiled. "I'm glad we had this conversation. Y'all seem cool. If you'd like to talk payment, we can have the weapons loaded for you."

Money was exchanged, and a couple of workers helped Scratch and Teddy load the crates onto the truck the Acosta brothers drove. Soon, they were gone, and Truck and Easy headed out to check the warehouses and the trap house before heading home. Then Romelo headed to his office to get his woman.

Sadie and Romelo shared an intimate dinner, in the movie room. They were kissing and cuddling with popcorn when Teddy came in.

"Boss? Someone's here to see you. I put them in your office."

"Teddy, why the fuck would you do that? I don't have an appointment with anybody."

"Yeah, but she—"

"She?" Sadie interrupted. Romelo sat up straight too.

Teddy cleared his throat nervously. "It's Bianca, Boss. Bianca's here."

Two

Bianca paced back and forth in Romelo's office, waiting for him to come in. She got into town two days before and kept herself busy settling things at the ballet school and moving into the apartment they'd given her as artist-in-residence. The school had very generous funders, so the apartment was roomy and updated, with two bedrooms, two bathrooms, and access to the private principal dancer studios. Bianca was pleased with the accommodation and felt confident about her new role. Her only worry was the school wanting her to revert to the more classical form of ballet dancing; there would be a learning curve as she adjusted.

"Bee?" The door to the office opened and Sadie walked in, her expression wary. Sadie was here. *Her* Sadie. Romelo walked in behind her and Bianca released a breath. They were both still so beautiful. Romelo with his big body, toffee eyes and delicious orange tints under his brown skin; Sadie with her light skin, always tinged with pink because she was always worked up about something, her cute little upturned nose, big eyes and round body. Bianca always thought of Sadie and Romelo as her very own Pooh and Piglet. Oh, how she wished she'd held onto them tighter.

They stood together, making no move to approach her. Bianca took a moment to register their body language. They were holding hands, Romelo standing behind Sadie like he was bracing her, supporting her. Sadie leaned into Romelo, trusting him. She was in her stocking covered feet, breasts loose under her blouse. Sadie was comfortable here... and half dressed. Did she live here?

"Hi," Bianca finally found her voice, clasping her hands together. Romelo and Sadie walked toward her, and she could feel their intimacy, practically smell their lovemaking. They were together now. The thought made her swallow hard. What if there wasn't room for her anymore?

"What are you doing here, Bee?" Romelo asked, getting straight to the point. Bianca was strangely comforted by his directness. He was still the same Romelo she knew. He didn't like his head played with, or his time wasted. He wanted the truth with the least amount of fanfare. The King didn't have the patience for games.

"I—I'm home. I've come home, and I needed to see you, see both of you—"

"Come home? For a visit? How long? What does that mean?" Sadie jumped in.

Bianca shook her head. "I'm home to stay. I got this great new opportunity, and I—"

"You're here to work?" Sadie pressed, interrupting again. Bianca was comforted by that as well. Sadie was impatient, impulsive, and prepped to fly off the handle. You had to get all the details out fast to keep her calm.

"No, Sadie—well, yes, I'll be working, but the job offer created the right set of circumstances for me to do what I've wanted to do for months. It gave me the chance to come back to you and apologize."

"Bianca—"

"Romelo please... let me get this out," Bianca begged. He nodded, moving to sit behind his desk. Sadie sat in his lap, staring like she wondered whether Bianca would say something about it. But what could she say? She left them both. They probably turned to each other when they couldn't find her, talked about the letters, consoled one another. Listened and cared for each other. Of course it turned into more. And Bianca could say nothing. She had no right.

"I was scared," she began, "I was scared out of my mind, and I made a rash, and hurtful decision. I left you both when you were the people who supported and loved me the most. I wouldn't have even had the courage to audition again for the company if you two hadn't believed in me. But when I got the spot, I thought I'd be holding myself back; I thought I needed to be unattached so I could focus on dancing and not what I was missing at home. I thought we'd be lonely and missing each other, and eventually you'd both move on, because you'd need more than I could give you. I ran away, like a coward—trying to leave you before you left me. Or before you got tired of waiting."

"Bee—"

"And I'm sorry," Bianca choked out, crying now, "I am so sorry. I love you still—both of you, and I am so fucking sorry for hurting you... for hurting all of us."

Bianca sobbed into her hands, humiliated. She wasn't supposed to lose her composure. She promised herself she'd be calm and mature. She sniffed, wiped her eyes.

"I didn't come here for this, I promise," she assured Romelo and Sadie, trying to get herself under control while they stared at her with eyes full of pity, "I know I was wrong. I'm not trying to get sympathy. I don't deserve your understanding, but I've needed to say this for a while, and it's been bottled up—"

"It's fine, Bianca," Romelo said, looking tortured. He never could stand to see her cry, "Try to take a deep breath. We're listening. It's okay—"

"But it's not!" she cried out, her tears refusing her directive to stop and continuing to pour down her face, "You're everything to me, and I've ruined it. Don't go easy on me, Ro. Nothing's okay about what I've done and I—" Bianca was crying too hard to continue now, sobs wracking her body.

She felt hands pulling on her arms, more hands pulling her up from the chair and suddenly she was surrounded, cocooned in the warmth of her loves as Sadie held her in front, and Romelo wrapped around her from behind. Bianca cried harder, relief nearly buckling her knees. They didn't hate her.

"We know why you left, Bee," Romelo whispered, rocking the three of them gently, "We know what getting a spot in the company meant to you. We never would have stood in the way of your dreams."

"We wish you had come and talked to us, let us *try* to work it out, but we understood. And we know you were scared. We know, baby," Sadie soothed.

"I didn't mean it," Bianca wailed, her shoulders shaking with her cries, "I didn't mean to hurt you. I swear, I'd give anything to take it back."

"Shhh. Hush now. You're gonna make yourself sick," Sadie soothed, holding her tighter. Romelo rubbed her back and Bianca felt equal parts, relieved and wary. She didn't deserve their kindness. But she needed it so badly.

"Let's all go into the living room and sit down. We have a lot to sort out, and we need to be comfortable," Romelo decided, pulling both Bianca and Sadie by the hand. Bianca followed meekly, not wanting anything to ruin the delicate truce they seemed to have. She glanced over at Sadie, holding Romelo's hand and staring at him with rapt adoration. *Did she ever look at me like that,* Bianca wondered. *Hell, did I ever look at Romelo like that?* The two of them were in perfect sync, it seemed. Obviously in love and very happy. Once again, Bianca's fear of there not being room for her anymore flashed across her mind.

The three of them situated themselves on the plush sofa, Romelo in the middle with Sadie and Bianca on either side. Sadie immediately leaned into him, her hand on his thigh. Bianca held back a sigh. She wanted Sadie's hand on her thigh. She wanted her hand where Sadie's rested. She wanted what Tanya and Charlie tried to give her. But she wanted it with her real loves, not their rebound understudies. Bianca felt a pang of guilt at her thoughts. Tanya and Charlie were good to her, patient and kind, and generous. But they were a faded version of Romelo and Sadie, a watered-down substitute for what her heart really wanted.

"As much as we can empathize with your tough decision, Bianca, the way you left us was unnecessarily cruel, and immature. Sadie and I were flailing, adrift without you," Romelo said, his deep voice sounding heavy and sad, as if he were back in the moment.

Bianca cleared her throat. "My letters—"

"Told us how much you loved us, how much you wished you could stay, how sorry you were, we know," Sadie cut in, "And we appreciated them. But those letters were full of shit we already knew. We *knew* how much you loved us, Bee. Which made what you did hurt even more. A person who loves me the way I *know* you love me, would let me try to make it work. You gave up for both of us without asking me, Bianca. You took away my choice—and Romelo's."

"I didn't—"

"Because given the choice, we would have chosen you, every single time, Bianca," Romelo said, taking a deep breath, "We would have come to you, flown you home when you had breaks, waited for you."

"But I didn't want you to have to do any of it. I was already splitting time between you. It felt like I was being greedy, asking for more compromise, more understanding, more flexibility—more from you, for *my* dream. I sacrificed to be able to dance; I knew it and signed up for that life. You didn't. Neither of you did," Bianca dragged a hand over her face and tried to explain. Her cheeks were still wet, and warm with guilt and sadness. Her two loves would have waited for her. They would have *waited*.

"We signed up to be with you, no matter what. You already know how I am, Bianca. When you get my heart, you get it forever."

Bianca nodded after Romelo finished. She was aware of how his heart worked. She'd never met a man more focused in his love than Romelo Davis. She supposed it was why she'd fallen so completely, and couldn't get up, even now. Bianca glanced up, watching Sadie look at Romelo like he was her every dream come true. And even with jealousy settling in her gut, Bianca understood. She felt the same way.

"You've apologized," Sadie said, turning to look at her, "What is it you want from us now?"

"Forgiveness... and another chance. I love you," Bianca said, taking a deep breath and looking across the couch, "I never stopped, and I never will. Please tell me what I have to do to show you I want you back, show you I'm here to stay. Tell me what I have to do to get you to look at me like you're looking at each other. Apologies mean nothing if I'm not willing to make amends. Tell me how to fix it."

After she spoke, Romelo and Sadie turned to each other, staring for a long moment. They seemed to be communicating something with their eyes, and Bianca was heartbroken to be on the outside looking in, and sad she didn't speak their language any-more. But she'd done this to herself. There was nothing left to do now but hope they let her fix things.

"We don't want you to fix anything, Bianca," Sadie said, and pain tore a gasp from Bianca's throat, "At least not in the way you think. Fixing implies we're putting what we had back together, and we can't."

Romelo picked up where she left off. "*If* we're doing this, we're building something new. I'm sure you can tell Sadie, and I aren't two acquaintances with the same girlfriend anymore. Shug and I are in love and devoted to our relationship. Our bond is solid. You're not the nexus of us anymore, Bianca, which means things will have to be different."

"I understand. I'm not between you anymore, and I can't try to be," Bianca agreed, relief making her breath explode from her chest. She thought they were dismissing her at first. Then she keyed in on Romelo's words. He'd given Sadie a nickname. His heart was invested, for sure.

"We want to rebuild trust with you, separately, but now we have the added task of doing it as a triad. We have to talk about rules, boundaries, and how to settle conflict. And I'm sure you've changed. You've been living your dream for the past year, and we need to know who you are now, and see you as you are now," Sadie said.

Bianca nodded. "There's so much I've missed about you two."

"First, we need to talk about whether you can handle, or would even consider being in a triad? When you were dating us sepa-rately, it never seemed like something you wanted."

"I thought about it a few times," Bianca answered Romelo, "But I didn't know if you and Sadie would want to get to know each other in that way. You seemed fine with your only connection being me. I guess I didn't want to rock the boat."

"But while I was away, I did explore a little. Before I came home, I was dating this married couple for a few months, Tanya and Charles Nance. They reminded me of you so much. I think it's why I gravitated to them. Being with them was like—it made me feel foolish for never asking you, because it was what I wanted all along."

"Do you still have feelings for them?" Sadie asked, sounding nervous.

Bianca shook her head. "They were wonderful to me, and I felt bad I could never return the affection they gave me so generously. But my heart was somewhere else, and they knew it. All three of us pretended not to see it, but we did."

"When you left them, did you explain why?" Romelo wanted to know. Bianca nodded again. There was no way she would make the same mistake twice. It was a hard conversation. Tanya cried, asked if there was anything they could do to make her stay. Charlie pointed out going home was a huge gamble, because she may not even get her loves back, but Bianca was firm. She belonged at home. Her heart was back home, whether Romelo and Sadie forgave her or not.

"Yes. I learned my lesson, Romelo. I know communication is important and I don't want to have a track record of denying people an explanation when they deserve one."

"I'm glad you're here, Bee," Sadie said softly, almost tentatively, "I missed you."

Bianca smiled. "I missed you too, Sadie. This job was a godsend. It brought me back to you."

"What is the job, by the way?" Romelo asked.

"The Greater American Ballet Company has opened their own school here," Bianca explained, "and they've asked me to be a principal dancer and artist-in-residence."

"Artist-in-residence? Oh Bee, how exciting!" Sadie said, clapping her hands in delight. Bianca grinned.

"Can y'all break it down for the civilian in the room?" Romelo laughed.

Bianca took his hand. It felt warm in hers, comforting. And he didn't pull away. "Principal dancer guarantees me a lead role in every major production. Artist-in-residence means I'll have input on the shows' concepts and choreography. Plus, I'll be teaching masterclasses and leading rehearsals and demonstrations. The school houses me and pays me a generous stipend, and barring sickness or injury, the job is guaranteed as long as the school is funded."

"It sounds like a damn good opportunity for you, Baby Girl," Romelo said. Bianca's gaze snapped to his. He called her... Baby Girl. His love name for her, the symbol of his affection, the name he whispered most when he was deep inside her and they were lost in each other. Bianca felt tears coming to her eyes. She was still his Baby Girl.

"It is," she said, her voice nearly a whisper. Her memory locked in the moment; she wanted to pause it and savor it, "It will be challenging going from the more freeform and looser dancing I've been doing, back to the tighter, more traditional movement of ballet, but it's going to be fun too."

"Oh, you know you've got it. I'm so excited for you. I'd love to see the school when it's open," Sadie said, practically bouncing on her side of the chair. Bianca giggled.

"I will come over tomorrow and pick you guys up, take you on a tour. Maybe we can get lunch after."

"Are you asking us on a date, Bianca?" Romelo's voice rumbled, amused.

Bianca shrugged. "You want to know who I am now, right?"

"Yeah," Sadie grinned, "We do."

"And I want to be with you. It's settled. 1:00pm okay?" Bianca said, standing up. She wished she didn't have to go, but she had meetings in the morning, and she liked to start her day with a warmup, even when she wasn't dancing in a show. *Besides*, she thought, *all three of us can use a breather after this conversation.* It was a little surreal, Romelo and Sadie giving her another chance, but Bianca wouldn't waste it. This time, she was home to stay.

"1:00pm is great. But you have to go right now?" Sadie said, standing up too. Bianca nodded.

"Yeah, I should. There are still boxes all over my apartment; I haven't even made the bed so I can get in it. Plus, y'all were obviously having a quiet night to yourselves. I won't interrupt anymore. I know quiet nights at home are hard to come by for you, Romelo."

"You're right, Baby Girl," Romelo said, a small smile on his lips, "Some things don't change. But I'm gonna have Teddy follow you home. I don't want you on these roads by yourself when it's dark."

"Oh, you don't have to—"

"Some things don't change, Bianca," Romelo said, putting up a hand to stop her. Bianca nodded. Romelo didn't play about their safety, not then and apparently not now. She gathered herself and they walked her to the door. Bianca turned to walk away, and then turned again, hugging them both tightly.

"Thank you," she whispered, feeling herself about to cry for the umpteenth time, "Thank you for listening to me, and accepting my apology. I'm going to show you what you mean to me. I promise."

"Thank you for following your heart home, Baby Girl," Romelo whispered back. Bianca sniffled. She backed up, smiling. Sadie leaned up on her toes, kissed her cheek.

"We'll see you tomorrow," she said, her eyes shining with tears. Bianca went to her car, another perk in her position, and got in, starting the engine and driving away. She plugged in her phone and started some music, comforted by Teddy's headlights in her rearview. She didn't have her loves back, but she had a chance. Now it was time to take the notes they'd given her, tighten up, and come hard. Because Bianca refused to lose them again.

Sadie

"She's still fine as hell and she smelled so good! Like, peaches and lilacs or something," Sadie was rambling as she kicked off her shoes. She was recalling every moment of her and Romelo's conversation with their former love—who they still loved. Bianca was still profoundly beautiful, her skin still a smooth deep warm brown. Her small eyes were black as night, and just as intense; Sadie found herself looking away before she lost herself in them. Her body was slightly more muscular, but still willowy and graceful, her movements soft, but powerful. She was still wide hipped with plump breasts that overfilled your mouth slightly. The only difference was her hair. Her kinky afro, formally a pineapple atop her head was now a bob length twist out, colored bright purple. It had taken Sadie's breath away to look at her, even as it filled her with unease and latent anger.

Sadie was a little surprised she didn't yell at Bianca, or rage against her carelessness in leaving them like she did. She could only guess it was because she'd had Romelo to pick her up when it happened, and it was clear Bianca had thrown herself into work to attempt to forget. _I had someone here to take care of me and nurse my_ *heart back to health,* she thought. *Bee had to go it alone, and suffer her own consequences. I definitely got the better end of the deal.*

Romelo sat on the edge of the bed, naked, waiting for her to finish undressing and lie down with him. He was smiling at her never-ending sentences, knowing her dreamy state was only making her move slower.

"Your jewelry, Shug," he said, reminding her she hadn't removed it. Sadie's hands went to her ears.

"Oh damn. Thank you, baby," she said, giggling a little. Her earrings dropped onto her vanity, then her diamond bracelet. Sadie shimmied out of her unfastened skirt and pushed down her panty hose. Her top was already gone, and she'd freed her breasts from her bra earlier, right after Truck and Easy left, "Anyway, she looked the same, but so different, you know? I was expecting to be angry when I saw her, but I wasn't, baby. I was a little angry, but it wasn't the all-consuming rage I thought it would be. And you could tell she really regretted what happened. You told me Bee would realize no one could love her better, and she did, babe! She even tried to replace us—and it didn't work! You were right and—"

"Shug, where's your bonnet?" Romelo interrupted, still smiling. Sadie turned in a circle, looking around the room. She didn't see her bonnet anywhere. She padded into the bathroom, looking at her sink, and then on the hook behind the door. Not seeing it, she ventured through the large bathroom to the walk-in closet, looking around. She spied her bonnet peeking out of the dirty clothes hamper. How the hell did it get in there? Frustrated with her own absentmindedness, Sadie rifled through her accessory drawers for a clean one and went back into the bedroom, pulling it over her braids. The light was off, and Romelo was in bed, sitting up. He was waiting for her. Sadie smiled. She got a running start since the bed was so high and climbed in, crawling to the middle and wrapping herself around her man. Romelo chuckled and pulled the blankets over them, and they finally moved into laying on their mountain of pillows.

"Are you really okay with us trying to trust Bee again?" Sadie asked Romelo. During the conversation, they'd read each other's cues and were able to convey the thoughts they were both having, but Sadie was still worried. She was excited to get to know Bee again, but this new dynamic would change things. She didn't want Romelo to think anything was changing regarding the way she felt about him. And she wanted to curb any jealousy she might have over Bianca's affection for him. She'd seen the way the other woman hung on his every word, and visibly relaxed whenever he smiled. Bianca was still as taken with Romelo as she'd always been, and why wouldn't she be? The man was *everything*.

"Yeah, Shug. I think the three of us can have something greater than we ever had dating her separately, and greater than any of us have now. And I don't want you to overthink my last statement because we're happy, Sadie Marie. You are my love, and my life. But neither one of us stopped loving Bianca, and we've never tried to hide it."

"I know. I know what you meant. You are my love, and my life. But Bee is a part of us, and we said if she ever came home, we'd give it a shot."

"No, I said *when* she came home," Romelo corrected, "I knew we matched Bianca in every way, and no one could compete with us. I was sure Bee was coming home. Because she'll never find anyone who knows her and can love her the way she needs."

"She had Tanya and Charles though," Sadie said, nervous, "You think it means something that she was able to ask them for what she wanted all along, but she never asked us?"

"I think when she was here with us, she always had someone, so she never had to explore it too deeply. When she didn't have either of us, she was finally able to articulate needing us both at once. And Tanya and Charlie were there to show her how it could be."

"But what if they want her back? They must have been great for her to spend months with them. What if—"

"The three of us will make things good again, and Bianca will stay. Nothing is taking Baby Girl away from us this time. I promise," Romelo said, kissing the top of her head. Sadie snuggled closer, even though she was practically in his skin already.

"You're calling her your Baby Girl again," Sadie whispered, smiling in the dark. The nickname always amused her whenever Romelo would use it around her. Bianca was so take-charge with her, so together, so fiercely independent—she'd balk at anyone even implying she needed coddling, so Sadie assumed she'd hate a nickname infantilizing her. But not when Romelo used it. Bianca leaned right into his care, softened like warm butter when he called her his "Baby Girl." Sadie was always amazed to see it.

"She is my Baby Girl, just like you're my Shug."

"I am your Shug. Our love is unshakeable, and with the three of us working together, we'll be complete." Sadie kissed Romelo's chest and buried her nose in his neck, breathing deep. Romelo's arms tightened around her, and they fell asleep.

Romelo

"Bianca? Your girl, Bianca? Bianca Bellamy?" Trevino "Truck" Davis said incredulously as they sat in Romelo's "war room" doing the count. It was early in the morning, and he and his two most trusted enforcers, his cousin Trevino and his best friend Elliott "Easy" Tanner, were counting money and talking territory changes and product distribution. The "war room" was really Romelo's unused dining room. He'd closed it off, secured it from outside threats and made it a perfect space for commiserating with his capos.

"Yup. Baby Girl came home, finally."

"You said she would," Easy nodded at him as he picked up a pile of bills and wrapped it. His own girlfriend Keona had recently come home after being away for two years. Her father, the Wolf, had been keeping her and their son prisoner in his compound. It was the last straw in a long line of offenses; Romelo declared the Wolf a dangerous liability and the crew got rid of him.

Romelo grinned. "I did say it didn't I?"

"What she say about why she left?" Truck continued, pulling a stack of money from the counting machine and pushing it toward Romelo.

"Nothing me and Sadie didn't already know. She thought she was sparing us being neglected, and she thought she was sparing herself the heartbreak of watching us get tired and walking away. We had a talk about her communication, and I reminded her who I am. The King don't say shit he don't mean, and I don't go back on my word," Romelo said. Truck and Easy nodded. They knew he stood on business—in life, and in love.

Romelo "King" Davis only ever had one goal—to rise above his circumstances, at all costs. Poverty was suffocating him, and when the streets offered a way to breathe, he took it. He didn't think of himself as particularly special, or even more ambitious than others. But he was more focused. Money was the goal, and selling drugs was the vehicle to achieve it. Romelo knew he wasn't a good person, not noble or morally righteous in any way. He was simply a man who made a way for him and his little cousin Trevino, since neither of them ever had a soft place to land. Sometimes he regretted slinging poison to make his mark and better himself; sometimes he regretted turning his cousin into the deadliest killing machine this corner of the world had ever known, but the alternative was poverty and death. And Romelo would not let life take him poor and broken, not him or Trevino. So, he stood on business. He was the King—focused, dependable, direct. He didn't bullshit, and the punishment for disrespect was swift, and harsh.

But Romelo did have a saving grace. He had a tender heart for the people he loved, the people he saw his future in. His one blessing was his ability to love wholly and without reservation. He'd fight for love, kill for love, defend it with his life. And once you had his heart, his devotion was unmatched. It was another thing he and Trevino had in common, and Trevino had two true loves to show for it, his girlfriend and boyfriend, Nasima and Bashir. Maybe Romelo would end up with two true loves as well.

"What you and Sadie gon do now? Y'all whole dynamic is different," Easy asked.

Romelo sighed. "It is, indeed. But there was always room for Bee; we just have to take our time and do this right. Make sure everyone has what they need."

Truck offered his advice. "In the beginning, Nas was afraid of causing friction between me and Butta every time she got attention from one of us and not both. She was walking on eggshells trying to balance some scale that didn't exist. You gotta make sure you nip that in the bud. Bianca needs to be comfortable leaning on either one of you at any time, without feeling like she's testing loyalties."

Romelo nodded in agreement. It was one of the first things he wanted to talk about, for his girls and for himself. The night before, watching the two women stare at each other longingly, reach for one another when they thought he wasn't looking, and become totally enraptured with one another, it stirred feelings of want and lust, but also feelings of jealousy. They had something he wasn't a part of, something lasting and strong. *We're going to need to talk this out with as much detail as possible*, he thought. Romelo didn't want there to be any room for doubt.

"And while I know the past is going to come up, don't harp on it too much. If you say y'all moving on, and starting new, then do it. Don't try to trip Bee up with the past. If you forgive her, and you want her in your life, act like it. Clean the slate. It's a lesson Key and EJ taught me." Easy said, referring to his woman and son while offering his own counsel. Romelo nodded again. He knew these two men knew what they were talking about.

"Good lookin' out. I appreciate y'all. This is a new road I'm walking down, but Bianca coming home, and then coming directly to me and Sadie was a sign: I don't see myself without either one of them, and I'll do what it takes to move us forward."

"Do y'all think it's strange, having all of our long-lost women come home like this?" Easy asked. The three men looked at each other, deep in thought.

"I think it's the best kind of coincidence. Like the universe knew we'd need more stability and love at this point in our lives," Truck replied.

Romelo smiled. "You might be right, cuzzo. This has been our most profitable year, and more money definitely brings more problems. Stakes are higher than they've ever been for us in the streets; no better time for our home lives to be peaceful and happy. And now they can be."

"Speaking of home lives, I climbed up out of some Grade A pussy to do this count early with you niggas. Let's wrap it up so I can go eat my woman for breakfast before the boy needs our atten-tion," Easy said, sitting up straight and getting them back on task. Romelo and Trevino laughed, and Romelo started separating and stacking money again, making notes in his ledger. He had to hurry too. He and Sadie had a date this afternoon.

Three

S "Since when is Trevino the kind of person who invites people over to his house?" Bianca asked as she and Sadie got into the car to wait for Romelo. He was standing outside with Dave and Malice, giving what looked to be very detailed instructions.

Sadie giggled. "Don't be fooled; he's still not. This is all Nasima."

"His first love, right?"

"Yup," Sadie nodded, "Since Nasima came home, he and Bash have been lighter, happier. She makes those two men *fold*, you hear me? Because of her, Bash doesn't walk around like he's about to square up with everyone, and Trevino? She takes *all* the bite out of his bark. The only thing that makes them revert is protecting her."

"I guess the right person can make all the difference," Bianca said, staring out of the window thoughtfully. Sadie hoped so. She hoped with all her heart the three of them could make things work, in a brand-new way. Bianca and Romelo silenced the noise better than anyone she'd ever been with. Romelo was firm and steady, indulgent and patient. Bianca was calming and encouraging, quiet and intense. Her daddy would say they were the sunlight and water her seed needed to grow.

Sadie Marie Wells was born in the South, to a Black cowboy who loved his woman, his land, and the family who helped them cultivate it. She was headstrong, impulsive, bossy, and stubborn, and her father and brothers thought she was perfect, which to her, was all the validation she needed. In her world, there were three rights no one was ever taking away: her right to own guns and shoot them, her right to throw hands for disrespect, and her right to fall in love. Sadie believed in love like she believed in stars and sunshine, and the healing power of horses. But she was a wild thing, a free spirit, a top who spun so fast no one was ever brave enough to come close—until Bianca Bellamy.

She met Bianca at the grocery store of all places, while she was trying to pretend her flaming hot cheesy popcorn was healthy, and Bianca was trying to pretend her plain popcorn was an indulgence. The two of them joked about switching and fell into a conversation, walking around the store together. A week later, Sadie forgot all about popcorn, because pretzels had become her snack of choice, and inspiration for how many ways she could fold up her flexible dancer girl in bed. They were a lightning strike together, a flame no one would put out, and Sadie was happier than she'd ever been.

When Bianca introduced her to Romelo, and said she was in love with him too, Sadie tried not to notice him. All men had shown her up to that point was she couldn't trust any except the ones she shared DNA with. But Bianca was in a perpetual state of bliss when she was with Romelo, so Sadie started looking closer, thinking maybe he was one she could give a pass, for Bianca's sake, of course. Bianca leaving forced her to open her eyes fully and see Romelo and as soon as they talked, as soon as they hugged, as soon as they kissed, Sadie knew why Bianca had fallen so hard for him. Romelo loved with his entire soul, and he made sure you could feel it. His devotion was unrivaled, his ability to listen and indulge was unparalleled, and his lovemaking was in a class by itself. Sadie still swooned on the daily, even after nearly two years of watching him with Bianca until she left, and months of being with him herself after she was gone.

"We ready?" Romelo said, getting into the car. Both Sadie and Bianca jumped, surprised to hear his voice.

"Y-yeah, babe. We're ready when you are," Sadie said, blinking away her memories.

Romelo stared intently. "You aight, Shug?"

"Yes, love. I'm fine. We can go," she said, grabbing his hand to reassure him. Romelo squeezed her fingers and then lifted her hand to his mouth, kissing it. He knocked on the partition with his other hand and they were off, to a backyard barbecue at Trevino's house.

It was their first public outing as a throuple. Their first date had gone almost ridiculously well, and they were all on a high from how seamless it was. Bianca showed them the school where she was working, and Sadie and Romelo were nearly as happy with her accomplishments as she was. Bianca also showed them her apartment, and she and Sadie oohed and ahhed over the modern decor and natural light while Romelo made mental notes on the safety and access. Once the tour was over, he took Bianca's spare key and called Trevino over to take it and implement some tougher security measures—installing hallway cameras, securing blind spots, and updating the locks. He also put a tracker on her car. The three of them dined in a private room at one of the nicest restaurants in town while it was happening, and they plied Bianca with questions about her year with the dance troupe. She thought the security upgrade was a bit extreme, and told them so, but Sadie knew it was necessary. The King's operation had grown in the year Bianca was gone, and he'd taken out the Wolf. Nothing could be left to chance, especially where their safety was concerned.

Bianca was thrust into work, so they'd had to wait some days for their second date, but it was just as enjoyable. The three went to dinner this time, at a jazz club with a live band. The noise level wasn't conducive to talking, so they kept it surface level, speaking about their general aspirations for their budding relationship while they enjoyed the music. They shared some kisses but hadn't taken it any further.

Today, they were meeting up with their family—Nas, Truck, and Bash, plus Easy and Keona and their little one—and it was the official coming out for their triad. Bee was home and they were back together, in a different way, but probably the best way. Sadie knew they would finally talk about expectations and boundaries after this date—it was time for them to dig in deeper.

"Sadie!" Nasima yelled as Romelo stepped out of the car and offered his hand to first her, and then Bianca, "You're here!" Sadie grinned and went to hug her friend. She and Nas had grown close in the months since the other woman had come home to her men. Nasima had grown up here, and was Trevino's first love, but they separated when she went away. A bad experience with her ex brought her home, and right back into Trevino's arms. He'd been in a relationship at the time, but his man Bashir had fallen just as hard for Nas, so they convinced her to stay and be with *both* of them. The three of them couldn't be happier now, and Sadie couldn't help but hope Bianca's return was her chance at the same happiness.

"Nas! I missed you, boo. You look good as hell!" Sadie replied as she and Nasima held each other tightly.

"You look kinda fine yourself, baby. And did you get new perfume? You smell delicious."

"What I tell you about flirting with my woman, Nas? You got two niggas already, damn," Romelo joked with a smile. Nasima laughed.

"Shut up, Melo, before I take her from you," Nasima joked back, throwing her hand on her hip. Romelo laughed and tugged Bianca forward.

"Nas, this is our... this is Bianca. Bee, this is Nasima, Trevino and Bashir's other partner," Sadie introduced. Bianca's eyes lit up, and Sadie knew she was more comfortable knowing they weren't the only throuple in attendance.

"The dancer, right? I've seen you perform. You're very talented, and it's great to meet you," Nasima said, with a smile. Bianca's smile was genuine and huge, and Sadie felt like the day was going to go well.

"You've seen me? I'm really flattered. It's great to meet you too. Your house is amazing."

"Thanks. Bash can speak more about it. It belonged to his grandparents—"

"Bring y'all asses on!" Trevino yelled from the front door, "The party is in the back, not by the damn car!"

"As you can hear, Trevino is still Trevino," Sadie said. The rest of them laughed and headed to the house. Another round of greetings and then they were in the backyard. It was set up with picnic tables with benches, padded patio chairs, with small tables next to them, and a fire pit. Bashir was pouring drinks and Romelo helped all the women settle into a comfortable seat before he went to the grill with his cousin. Sadie licked her lips, watching him. He was dressed simply—a gray tee, matching lightweight joggers, and some exclusive sneakers she'd never heard of, but his fresh haircut, and gold link chain complemented perfectly, and he looked positively edible to Sadie.

"Don't you just want to lick him?" Bianca whispered to her, and she turned, nodding.

"He looks so good, I can barely keep still," Sadie said, happy she only felt consensus with Bianca's statement, and not jealousy.

"The worst part is he's completely oblivious," Bianca went on, "You'll be making a mess in your panties, and he'll be shrugging his shoulders like he has no idea what you're so excited about."

"Exactly!" Sadie said, and the two of them giggled. Romelo turned to look at them, winking and blowing them a kiss before turning back to the grill.

A few minutes later, Bashir went to the front and came back with Easy, his girlfriend Keona, and their adorable baby, EJ. Sadie and Bianca had been around when Keona disappeared, and she and Romelo filled Bianca in on why she left.

"Bianca?" Keona spoke. Bianca smiled and stood up, moving to hug Keona.

"Hey Key. It's so good to see you again," she said. Sadie stood up too, scooping EJ up from where he stood beside Keona holding her hand and kissing her cheek as she walked away with him.

"Hey girl. Give me my baby," she said, tickling his belly. EJ laughed.

Easy grunted. "Boy ain't never gon walk, y'all keep carrying him. And you can't speak now, Sadie?" Sadie giggled and backtracked, giving Easy a hug with one arm.

"Hey Easy. Get some snacks in you, stop being so grumpy," she laughed.

Keona laughed as well. "I told him he needed to eat, his grouchy ass."

"Whatever, man. Let my shorty walk; he need to get better at it, work on his balance," Easy threw over his shoulder, heading to the picnic table where Bashir was helping Nasima put out chips and crackers with dip and salsa, a fruit plate sitting on a bed of ice, and cucumber salad. Romelo and Trevino were grilling vegetables and flatbreads first, before any meat touched the grill. Sadie took EJ to the other side of the yard where Nasima had set up a play area for him with blankets and toys, and a mini ball pit.

"Is this a hard launch?" Keona asked, following. Sadie put EJ down in the ball pit and he threw himself backward, laughing hysterically as the balls covered him.

"Yeah... I guess it is," Sadie replied, smiling softly, "We're still working things out, but me and Melo want it to be clear Bee is part of us again, and part of this family again. We can't make her stay, but we can make damn sure we're not the reason she leaves this time."

"You weren't the first time, Sadie. We all make our own choices about things. Sometimes we don't want to confront our fears. But it's not on you to figure out another person's hang-ups. Take it from someone whose man constantly wonders what he could have done differently—the answer is nothing. All you can do is move forward—you and Romelo."

"I know you're right, Key. I know it. But when does it stop feeling so fragile? Like one wrong move will break it? I want it like it was before."

"But it's not like before Sadie, and it won't be," Keona pointed out, getting down on the ground to gather EJ's sneakers, since he'd gotten out of them, "New is scary, and it feels fragile because it *is*. As for when it stops, honestly... I'll let you know."

"Key—"

"Easy says he believes in me, and in us. He says I can relax. But his heart and his faith are precious. And after he chased away every monster in my life, all I want to do is show him he can trust me with them. He says I don't have anything to prove, but I can't help feeling like I do."

"I know Bianca feels like she does. But I do too, in a way. I want to show them I can handle loving both of them; I was *made* to love both of them. They're mine, Key, and I don't want either of them questioning where they belong. They belong with me," Sadie declared. She sat down on the grass with her friend, and they watched EJ flop around and throw balls in the air, amusing himself. Sadie stared over at Bianca, her outfit plain but still sexy—soft gray leggings, an oversized graphic t-shirt Sadie suspected she'd stolen from Romelo long ago, and high top 1s. She realized her two loves were matching. It made her smile.

Keona smiled. "Look at you. You can't keep your eyes off them. Listen, it'll all work out. We'll show and prove and make each other strong."

Sadie leaned into her as they sat side by side. "Thanks, baby."

Bianca

Bianca spread creamy garlic dip on a flatbread and topped it with grilled peppers, sliced portobello mushrooms, and zucchini strips. She folded her flatbread and took a huge bite, closing her eyes and dancing a little. Two bites later, it was done, and she was contemplating another. She was having such a good time. There was music, conversation, great food, cards, dominoes, and the drinks were flowing. She made a mental note to thank her hosts; she knew the abundance of veggies and seafood was at least partly because Romelo told them she limited her meat consumption when she was dancing every day. Meat was heavy, and it sometimes made her feel too sluggish.

Sadie handed her a wineglass, refilled like she'd asked. "You okay?"

"Yes, baby. I'm fine," Bianca reassured her. After Sadie's talk with Keona, she'd gone to Romelo and kissed him over and over, whispering something to him as she stood in his arms. Then she'd come over to Bianca and kissed her, telling her between soft, juicy, pecks how happy she was they were all together again. Bianca had been left stunned, overcome and emotional, her lust rising fast. Sadie still took her breath away. She sipped her wine, licking her lips in remembrance.

"What you thinking about?" Sadie asked. Bianca turned to her, smiling.

"How good your lips taste," she shrugged, like it was no big deal. Sadie blushed to her ears, grinning with delight. Bianca loved when she was shy like this, when she acted like she had no idea how sexy she was. She leaned over, kissed Sadie's neck, sucked on the soft skin gently. Sadie gasped, her eyes closing as she tilted her head to give her better access. Bianca kissed her again and again, loving the way her breaths sped up and she balled her little hands into fists, as if she was trying to keep from reaching for her. Suddenly Romelo sat on the other side of Sadie and kissed her neck too, his arm going across the back of their chairs. Sadie moaned out loud, gasping a little.

"Sharing you is going to be so much fun, Shug," Romelo whispered to them both. Bianca stared at him, her nipples hardening. Sadie finally unclenched her fists and pushed them both away, breathing hard.

"We are putting on a show, and y'all will not have me walking around here with soaked panties for the rest of the day."

"Ain't nobody paying us no mind," Romelo said casually, sitting back in his chair and swirling his whiskey. The two women turned to him, smiling. He was magnificent, thick and sturdy with his big brown eyes and sun kissed skin and freshly cut hair. His large hand wrapped around his glass, and his thick lips kissed the edge of it as he took easy sips of his drink. Bianca wanted to climb into his lap, and she knew by the way Sadie was still a bit breathless, she was thinking the same thing. Bianca's lustful thoughts were halted by the buzz of Romelo's cell phone. He sighed, standing up and removing it from his pocket as he walked away to talk.

"What?" Bianca heard him say, his impatience evident. She leaned into Sadie and looked around at the party again. Their family guest list had grown to include Linc and Bunky, the two guys who managed Bashir's boxing gym in town; Elliott's grandmother, who everyone called MomMom, and Scratch and Teddy, Romelo's personal bodyguards.

"Sadie? Let me holla at you for a second," Easy said, walking over to them. Sadie nodded and hopped up, following him to a corner of the yard where Trevino was waiting. The three of them spoke, their heads together, faces serious. A moment later, Romelo was off the phone and over in the corner with them, seemingly giving them an update. Bianca frowned. She knew Romelo's call was business, so it made sense he'd be updating Easy and Trevino. What was Sadie doing over there? Romelo had never discussed business with her, or even where she could hear him. Why was Sadie different?

"I thought you might like some before it's gone," Nasima walked up with a plate of perfectly grilled salmon and two shrimp skewers. Bianca started, pulling her attention from whatever was happening in the corner of the yard.

"Oh, um—thanks. Thank you, Nas," she said, smiling. Nasima sat the plate on the small table beside Bianca and looked over to where Bianca had been staring.

"I'll go break them up. Work is forbidden today—Vino promised," she assured her and walked away. Bianca sighed.

Nasima thought she was upset they were talking about work on Family Day. But her comment confirmed Bianca's suspicion. They had been discussing business—*with* Sadie. Since when did Sadie work for the organization? And why would Romelo allow it? He was adamant, damn near obsessive, about keeping her away from his street life. The only information he ever gave her was about things relevant to her safety. Why would he bring Sadie all the way in? Did he trust her more? Or care for her less? It didn't make sense.

"Oh good, Nas brought you the salmon. You want some more veggies?" Sadie said, sitting back down and kissing her cheek. Bianca turned, wanting to ask Sadie why she was working with Romelo, and how long it had been going on. But the words stuck in her throat. She'd been gone for a year. Did she even have the right to question them? *They wanted to know everything about what I've been doing,* Bianca thought, *why wouldn't they tell me this?*

"Bee? Hello? Where'd you go? I asked you a question," Sadie said, waving a hand in front of her face. Bianca shook her head, snapping out of her haze.

"I'm sorry. What did you ask me?"

"I asked if you wanted veggies to go with your salmon and shrimp. Are you okay?"

"Y-yeah, I'm fine. I-I'm good. I'll get some pasta salad and another piece of flatbread when I get up. Don't worry about it."

"I'll get it for you, baby. I don't mind. You sure you're okay?" Sadie said, stroking her cheek. Bianca swallowed. She closed her eyes, leaning into Sadie's touch. This was still her Sadie. *Her* Sadie.

"Hurry back, okay?" she said, her voice soft. Sadie nodded and got up again, going to the next table and getting her pasta salad and a flatbread slathered in dip. She also got another plate with barbecue chicken, mac and cheese, macaroni salad, and corn.

Bianca watched her say something to Romelo and incline her head toward where she was waiting. Romelo nodded and Sadie came back over. Bianca sighed.

"Here we go," Sadie said, sitting the two plates down before getting comfortable in her chair.

"What did you tell Romelo?" Bianca asked, trying to keep the accusation from her voice. She wasn't angry, but she couldn't help wondering what else they were keeping from her. Sadie stared at her, frowning.

"I told him we needed drink refills, and he should get a plate and come eat with us," she answered, shaking her head and picking up her chicken. Bianca opened her mouth, ready to apologize, explain—she didn't know what. Sadie obviously picked up on the edge in her voice. Bianca didn't want to fight; she wanted to understand why Romelo was willing to throw Sadie into a situation he'd avoided with *her* at all costs, and why neither of them thought to tell her.

"Two refills for my ladies," Romelo announced, balancing two glasses and a plate. He sat on the other side of Sadie where he was before, putting the glasses on the small table in front of him. Bianca picked up her glass, taking a healthy sip. Sadie frowned again.

"I knew you weren't fine—what's going on with you?" she asked. Bianca turned to her.

"What do you mean?"

"That's not your glass, Bee. It's mine, and it has rum punch in it, not wine, which is what you were drinking. You didn't even register it. What's wrong?" Sadie replied. Romelo stopped eating, staring over at her too. Bianca sighed.

"How long have you been working for Romelo?" she blurted out, stuffing salmon into her mouth after as if it could stop her from saying more words. She chewed as they looked at each other, and then back at her. They were communicating something with their eyes again, speaking to each other in a language she didn't know anymore. Bianca felt awkward and left out.

"We should talk about this later, when we get to the house," Romelo finally said, reaching over and wiping the sauce from the salmon from the side of her mouth with his thumb. Bianca nodded and dropped her eyes. They probably needed time to get their story straight and decide how much to tell her.

"Right. Later," she mumbled. Romelo put his plate down and got up, moving in front of her. He dropped into a squat and grabbed her chin, lifting her head.

"Fix your face," he ordered, his voice going low and forceful. His eyes narrowed and he tilted his head, waiting for her to obey him. Bianca did, her heart racing and her panties dampening. She licked her lips, relaxing her face and looking into his eyes.

"Sadie and I weren't trying to keep anything from you, Bee. We have to be very careful about who knows, and there's more to it than you think. And now is not the time, nor is Trev's backyard the place for us to have this conversation. Do you understand me?"

"Yes, baby," she whispered, feeling both scolded and turned on. Her body was hot, sensitive, and between her thighs she felt achy and sticky. Romelo kissed her lips and stood up again, going back to his food. Bianca sat back and resumed eating her pasta salad.

"I could never shut you up so easily," Sadie threw out, smirking as she forked macaroni salad and put it in her mouth.

"Oh hush," Bianca said, her cheeks warm. She was still curious about Sadie working with Romelo and was dying to have her questions answered. But he was right about it not being the appropriate time or place. And Sadie was right about Romelo's effect on her. When he was dominant and commanding, drawing on the same energy he used to run his streets with an iron fist, he was King of the world, and King of her too.

Romelo

Romelo sat back in the car, relaxing his body. His eyes closed and his hands reached out. Sadie grabbed one, and Bianca the other. They both leaned against him, lifting his arms and snuggling into his sides. He held them both as they drove to his home. Family Day was tiring, but ultimately worth it. When Trevino first told him Nas wanted to invite everyone over, he was skeptical. Then he realized a backyard barbeque was normal for most families. He'd never thought of it because those things never happened in the family he and Trevino came from. But today there was food, drinks, cards and dominoes, and even an interesting roundtable discussion about marriage. EJ ran himself ragged, despite being the only kid there, and even Scratch and Teddy cracked a smile. They were in the car ahead of him now; it was their job to make sure the house was secure before he arrived. A few minutes later, they pulled up in front of his door, a Tudor-style mansion with pitched roofs and authentic stonework. Bianca sat up, stretching.

"Oh good, we're here. I have to go to the—" Romelo yanked her back from the door handle.

"You know Scratch and Teddy have to clear it before we go in," he told her. Bianca nodded, as if she'd only just remembered. Romelo knew along with exploring the boundaries of their new relationship dynamic, he'd also have to refresh Bianca on the rules. Their safety was paramount, and with so much growth in the operation, he couldn't have anything slipping.

Scratch opened the car door, giving him the nod and then taking Bianca's hand to help her out of the car. She disappeared into the house while he and Sadie got out. Sadie tugged on his shirt, making Romelo stop and look down at her.

"Baby, I don't know about telling someone else," she said. Romelo sighed. He knew this part was going to be hard for them, mostly because this wasn't a recent secret Sadie was keeping. But they had to go through with it. The two of them agreed it was time for Bee to know.

"This is how we show her we trust her, Shug. It isn't going to work if we're not honest."

"I know," Sadie said and walked inside. She headed into the house, and he followed. Romelo went to his office, checking his other cell phone quickly. He sent Trevino a text and headed to the living room, pouring whiskey when he got there. Sadie was on the couch, one leg tucked under her, tapping away on her cell phone. She wore a dress today, a short sleeved, low cut, red thing made of some stretchy material that clung to her juicy titties but then flared out over her belly. The dress stopped at the middle of her big thighs and with the way her ass poked, the back was up even further. Romelo couldn't wait to take it off her. The red Converse she'd worn with it were on the floor in front of the couch.

"I'm going to have a glass of wine. Sadie, you want one?" Bianca said, poking her head into the living room. Sadie looked up, nodding. Bianca was back moments later, two empty glasses and an opened bottle in her hands. She sat on the couch and filled the two glasses, passing one to Sadie. Romelo sat in the wingback chair across from them.

"Bianca, let me start this discussion by saying things have changed. Not only with us, and our relationship, but with the organization. We've grown substantially since you left, and we finally eliminated a threat we've had on our radar for years. Things are shifting with the business, and we've had to become even more selective about what we tell, and who we tell it to."

"You don't trust me anymore," Bianca replied to Romelo, her face falling.

"It's more complicated than that," he corrected her, "Everything has to be measured against whether it's safer for you to know or not know."

"I don't know if I can believe safety is your main concern when you'd let Sadie get involved with what you do, Melo. You'd never let me anywhere near your business. Why change your values now?"

"Bee, it's not—"

"I always admired your old school edicts of women and children being untouchable. You used to tell me you'd never taint me with the streets. But doing it to Sadie is okay? You said you loved her!" Bianca said, her voice rising. Romelo growled and looked away, trying to get his temper under control.

"You questioning my values now, Bianca? My love? You don't get to judge me. You. Weren't. Here. And Sadie means more to me—"

"—than I did? You trust her more, love her more? You're certainly not showing it!"

"Stop it!" Sadie yelled. She sat her wine on an end table and stood up, "Bianca, you are out of line. Romelo isn't 'letting' me do anything. I make my own decisions; I always have. His values haven't changed, and you owe him an apology. If you're angry with me, be angry with *me*."

"But he could have said no, Sadie! If I'd come to Romelo and asked him to move bricks, or push weight, or whatever the fuck it is, do you think he'd give me a job? No matter what you wanted, he should have shut it down!" Bianca yelled back. This conversation was spiraling, and Romelo wasn't sure how to save it. He didn't know whether Bianca was defending Sadie or lambasting him for not giving her the same level of trust, and he suspected she didn't know either. He opened his mouth to speak, but Sadie was faster.

"Why? I'm a grown woman! Romelo doesn't own me, Bee! He loves me, and he keeps me safe. You've got this all wrong. If you'd calm down and listen—"

"To what? Your Bonnie and Clyde stories? You gon tell me how y'all evaded the cops or met somebody in a dark warehouse? You gonna show me your tattoo, or your chain, or whatever you have that says you belong to the club?"

"It's more than you have," Sadie shot back, her face reddening with anger, "Isn't it? You don't have anything saying you belong here, and you're pissed about it."

"Sadie don't do this. We're getting off track—" Romelo started, but Bianca raised her hand.

"No, don't cut her off, Melo," she said, "Let her keep going. I never thought you were the type to buy into the whole 'ride or die bitch' persona, but I guess I don't know either of you anymore."

"Are you angry I've decided to be his ride or die, or angry you never had the chance to be?"

"Go to hell, Sadie!" Bianca yelled.

"Enough!" Romelo roared, finally silencing his two girlfriends. He clenched his fist and took a healthy sip of whiskey. This whole situation was madness, and he could feel a migraine coming, a dull ache that was going to be piercing in a very short time. And it was too late to take medicine; he'd been drinking all day. He'd be no good to anyone once it set in, so he needed to make things clear before his head took him out of commission.

"First—both of you owe *each other* an apology. The entire argument was childish, and unnecessary. Second, I didn't make Sadie join the organization, nor do I need a 'ride or die bitch.' She doesn't have a chain, or a tattoo, she's never pushed, moved, or evaded anything, and she's never been to my gotdamn warehouse. My values have never changed where women and children are concerned, *especially* women I love. And I love Sadie. Third, Bianca has never had cause to think or feel like she doesn't belong with me. She doesn't need anything to prove she's mine—or yours, Sadie. We clear?" The boom of his voice echoed through the room, and the two women sat there, looking sad at their fight, and embarrassed he was basically scolding them.

"Yes, Romelo," they both replied. Romelo sighed and took another pull of his drink.

"Lastly, as far as the business, Sadie works with me because I owed a favor to a friend. Her being good at what she does makes this easy. Simple as that."

"A favor?"

"Yes," Sadie confessed, moving to sit closer to Bianca. Romelo hated forcing her hand, but soft pedaling this wasn't working anymore. Sadie cleared her throat, "My grandfather heads the family who's been supplying Romelo for years. No one knows who I am to him, for my protection. After you left, he warned me an enemy of his had made his way to this area of the country. He asked Romelo to look after me."

"He didn't know I already knew who she was through you," Romelo jumped in, "It actually made things easier, because I could protect Sadie without people asking too many questions. Three or four months after you left, someone broke into her apartment, and she moved in here with me."

"Sadie, are you—"

"I'm fine, baby," Sadie interrupted Bianca and reached for her hand to soothe her, "I wasn't even home. And it turned out to be some random thief, but Romelo didn't want to take any chances. Once I lived here, I started showing Romelo all I knew about guns and equipment. He let me work because no one does this better than I do, and I need to keep busy. And because we got involved, it was seamless."

"Outsiders don't know Sadie as anything other than my girl-friend and I am very careful to keep her safe and out the way," Romelo said. Bianca sighed. She looked at them both, her eyes sad and shamed.

"I'm sorry," she said softly, "I am so sorry. I acted out because I'm jealous. You two have so many things I'm not a part of any-more. And it's been so good being with you, I guess I'm in a hurry to be in your bubble again. But I shouldn't have accused you and said those things. I shouldn't have questioned your integrity—either of you."

"I shouldn't have said those things to you, either. I was angry, and shit got out of hand," Sadie apologized. The two women kissed gently, smiling afterward. Romelo finished his drink and sat back, letting his body relax against the plush chair. His eyes closed briefly.

"We need to have a serious talk about our relationship rules. Because this is the last time I will *ever* referee between you," Romelo told them. Bianca and Sadie nodded in agreement.

"Let's have the talk tomorrow, baby. I can tell from your face you're in pain. Come on, we should lie down," Sadie said, looking over at him with alarm. Romelo conceded, standing up.

"It's a migraine, isn't it? And you can't medicate because you've been drinking," Bianca said knowingly. She and Sadie stood up too.

"Stay the night, Bee," Romelo asked, the pain in his head ratcheting up, "Come lay with us."

Bianca looked stunned. "A-Are you sure?" she asked. Romelo reached for her hand.

"Positive." She grabbed his hand, and the three of them went to bed.

Four

Sadie

Sadie sighed with pleasure as she watched Bianca spin and leap on stage. The opening show for the ballet company was scant weeks away, and spending time with her dancer girl was difficult with rehearsals, classes, and all her meetings about set design, formations, and costumes. Sadie decided to come and see Bianca, and hang out in her world, because she missed her, and because she wanted to show that her dreams mattered, and they always had.

Dancing was embedded into the very fabric of Bianca's existence, having done it since she was four years old. She probably loved it more than Sadie loved guns, which was saying something. And while dancing wasn't something that captured Sadie's attention, or even Romelo's, Bianca's passion for it demanded everyone around her notice. Her loves took heed, immersing themselves in the finer points of modern ballet and contemporary dance, sitting in the front row for all of Bianca's shows and watching their girl twirl with precision, and moving so beautifully it was impossible not to be pulled in. And the same was true today. Sadie was riveted; her mind locked into the talented, purple-haired goddess who was performing art with her body.

"Stop! Bianca, you're leaning too heavily into the turn. It's supposed to look effortless, ethereal—not like you're weighed down by your breakfast!" the director yelled from the front row. Bianca came to a stop, her forehead creased with annoyance. She sighed, nodded, and took several deep breaths.

"I'm thinking about it too hard. I'm sorry; let's go again," she conceded. Someone handed her a bottle of water, and she took three hefty gulps before handing it back. Then she stretched her arms high above her head, rocking her head from side to side to loosen her muscles. Sadie frowned. Her hand grasped the switchblade she'd hidden in the fabric of her skirt. Yelling at her dancer girl made Sadie want to cause a funeral, but Bee already told her she couldn't get violent every time someone corrected her.

"They're supposed to critique me, my love," Bianca had said to soothe her ruffled feathers after the first time Sadie came to rehearsals. She'd been lounging against Sadie's chest while her legs were stretched over Romelo's lap. He was rubbing her calves, ankles, and feet while he watched sports on TV. He'd been working all day and only showed up in time to take them to dinner.

"You're perfect, and they can correct without having so much condescension and bass in their voices," Sadie protested. Bianca had giggled, relaxing into her girlfriend's ample bosom.

"Sadie, as much as I love your willingness to shed blood to defend me, I can handle it. They have to be hard on me. My last dancing gigs were looser, and much less disciplined. They're helping me retrain my body, baby. They're the best in the business, and they don't mean anything by it."

Sadie calmed after her answer then, but sitting here now, watching and hearing their loud corrections, made her feel stabby all over again. The music came in from the top, and Bianca got into position. Her body moved at the right moment, sensual and fluid, almost as if someone else were controlling it. Sadie was mesmerized. Bianca went into the turn that made the director stop and Sadie leaned in, hoping she was projecting confidence and love onto her sweet dancer girl. Bianca was poetry in motion, all sinewy arms and spinning legs. When she finally came out of the turn and went into the rest of the routine, even the director sat down and shut his mouth. Sadie sighed, loosening her grip on the switchblade. It was always a good day when she didn't have to hurt someone.

"Can you believe they didn't even make her lose the dance troupe weight? Her ass is everywhere!" A whisper from behind made Sadie pay attention. Her fingers tightened on the blade again. Another woman giggled.

"Don't be mean, Thea. Bee's still got it."

"She's alright, I guess. If you like that sort of 'thickness.' But ballet is about looking delicate and weightless. No one is going to see those hips and think she's delicate. And do I detect some flab in her belly?"

"No, but I detect a hating ass bitch," Sadie said, turning in her seat, knife in hand. The two women gasped, backing away from her weapon and her anger.

"I—we—what are you—" the one she guessed was Thea sputtered, her eyes wide with fear.

"Say one more thing about my woman's ass, and your blood is gonna be everywhere."

"Okay Bianca, I think that's enough for today. Good job, hon. Thea, Melissa, you're up! I want to see your intro to the second act, and I hope you applied the notes I gave you yesterday!" the director yelled, interrupting Sadie's mission to keep her baby's name out of these heffa's mouths.

"Coming Marcel!" they yelled in unison and ran away, the relief dropping their shoulders and hurrying their steps. Sadie put her blade away in time for Bianca to walk up to her, bag over her shoulder, shoes in hand.

"You ready?" she asked, smiling wide.

Sadie nodded, trying to look as innocent as possible. "Yeah. You hungry, baby?"

Bianca stared into her eyes. Then she sighed and shook her head.

"Do I want to know what you've done?" she asked.

Sadie smiled brightly. "Maybe?"

Bianca laughed. "Tell me over food."

The two of them headed back to Bianca's apartment so she could change. They were meeting Romelo at a restaurant where he'd been having a meeting with some of his affiliates. He promised to be finished with business and at their table waiting with wine by the time they got to him. Bianca was barely inside the door before she was stripping her clothes off, hurrying to shower and change.

"I won't be long," she promised, going into the bedroom. Sadie licked her lips, her body coming to attention. She wanted to follow Bianca, rub on her firm ass, suck on her sensitive nipples. But they were holding all sex until their relationship was more solid, and it was understood their first time would be together. It was Sadie's own idea, and it was a good one... until she had to watch Bianca or Romelo undress in front of her. Her loves were so sexy it was almost painful to look and not touch. But she had to. She believed it would make them stronger to cement things emotionally first, before getting swept up in what Sadie knew would be mind-blowing sex. This was the way. But standing in the doorway of Bianca's bedroom, watching her dancer girl moisturize her perfect body after her shower, Sadie couldn't help but have second thoughts. *Shit*, she thought, reaching for her switchblade, *I need to stop carrying this before the frustration makes me stab somebody after all.*

<u>Romelo</u>

"You ain't getting no action at all? Like, not even hands and mouths?"

"Truck, ain't that what the fuck I said?" Romelo snapped, his patience low. It had been a long few weeks. Bianca was gearing up for the company's opening show, so she was rehearsing, and teaching, while also consulting on costumes, choreography, and set design. Sadie was researching buyers and processing a brand-new shipment of stolen Sig Sauer P229's, making sure they were stripped of all identifying markings and numbers, which was no easy task since they were government issue. Sometimes, even the inside of the clip or barrel was marked so the shell casings would have certain grooves after they were fired, so the work to check and clean everyone was detailed. Sadie was begging to keep one or two, but Romelo was selling them all; their armory was full, and nobody needed that many guns, not even his trigger-happy girlfriend.

"Wait, my nigga. I'm confused. You sleep with Sadie every night. Y'all ain't fucking either?"

Romelo grunted after Easy spoke. "Sadie thinks we should *all* wait, since technically, we're all in a brand-new relationship. She says since the two of us already live, work, and sleep together, we're doing so many intimate things Bee isn't part of, so continuing to have sex would be rubbing it in her face."

"Meanwhile, one of them should be rubbing it in your face," Trevino laughed, picking up a stack of money. Romelo scowled and he got himself together, "Look, my bad cuzzo. But real shit, while I get what Sadie's trying to do, it ain't like y'all strangers. All of you have had each other already. I don't see the big deal."

"Shit, neither do I. But my women do, and I'm riding with them. Ain't shit else I can do."

Truck and Easy shrugged after his statement, going back to the money. The three of them were on the early morning count again, getting things straight so Easy could pay their auxiliary staff. Dealers kept a quarter of what they made, but Easy oversaw paying everyone else: the runners, guards, shooters, bag boys, plus the warehouse and stash house workers, and the clean-up crew. Most organizations contracted clean-up and debt collection out to separate crews, but a few years before, Romelo brought all those things in-house, for efficiency. There were a lot more people to watch over, but it was worth it in terms of the money they saved, plus it was easier to weed out a rat.

The counting machine beeped, and Truck stared at it, frowning. He picked up the stack of money he'd put in the machine, counted it by hand, and then put it back in the machine. The machine finished counting and the number on the display made him frown deeper.

"E, did you take this bag from Dave yourself?" Truck asked. Romelo looked up, paying attention to the anger in his cousin's voice.

Easy shook his head. "Nah, he came out the house as I was pulling up and put the bag in the backseat. Why?"

"Cause it's short," Truck replied. Romelo scowled. Dave and Malik, or "Malice", were right underneath Truck and Easy in the hierarchy, street lieutenants who ran the corners on opposite sides of the city. Both had climbed through the ranks together, two friends who wanted the same thing: to run the city and make money. But over the years, Malice had outgrown his counterpart, taking on more responsibility in the organization, creating and introducing new avenues for revenue, and proving himself worthy of more trust. If Dave was jealous, he didn't let on, although something told Romelo, giving him a short bag was the first step to Dave showing his hand.

"Short by how much?" Romelo asked quietly.

"Two stacks," Truck answered.

"I'll get Dave here," Easy said, pulling out his cell phone. Romelo sat back, his hand going to his chin. Dave had never been short before, so it was weird for it to happen now, and for seemingly no reason. There was nothing new going on and things had been quiet. *Maybe too quiet?* he thought.

"I can get to the bottom of it for you, cuzzo," Truck said, starting to stand. Being Chief Enforcer meant disciplinary problems went through him. Romelo grabbed his cousin's arm, made him sit down again.

"It's cool. Dave can deal with all three of us now, and he'll know it ain't no second chances," Romelo said.

Easy put his phone away. "He's on his way," he mumbled. Romelo guessed he was blaming himself for accepting the bag without testing the weight of it. But Romelo knew Easy was solid, and this was on Dave.

"What you see when you pulled up to the trap? Anything stick out?" he asked. Easy nodded, closing his eyes so he could remember. Elliott "Easy" Tanner was otherwise known as "The Watcher," because of his ability to not only see without being seen, but also to recall everything his eyes captured.

"Someone was moving in across the way," he said, "And it's not really the kind of block people move *onto*, you feel me? Usually, people trying to get off the mufucka. The U-Haul had me stuck for a minute. Dave came out, threw the bag in, tapped the hood, and I pulled off again. I hit up Keys to see if he could find out who bought or rented the house, but I haven't heard back yet." Langston Jones, known as Keyboards or Keys, was their technical specialist and hacker. His role in the organization was mostly background intel, security analysis, and information gathering. Romelo needed to know who was around him at all times.

There was a knock at the door, and then Scratch stuck his head in. "Boss, Dave's here."

"Send him in," Romelo replied. Dave Walker entered the room, looking cool, and calm.

"You wanted to see me, King?" he spoke, nodding his head at Truck and Easy.

Romelo smirked. "It seems you forgot to give me something."

Dave stared at them, confused. "Forgot what?"

"The bag you gave me was light," Easy jumped in, "Two stacks missing. What happened?"

Dave's eyes widened. "I don't know nothing about that, King. The money was all there when I gave it to Easy."

"At this point, I don't really care. It's still on you. Just know you have 24 hours to find out who shorted you, and subsequently me, and bring them to Truck," Romelo said, standing up. He walked closer to Dave, looking for changes in his demeanor—faster breaths, eyes darting left to right, involuntary movement. Dave seemed normal, but his hands shook a little in his pockets and he shifted from foot to foot as Romelo got closer.

"Yo, King man, you know I respect you. I'd never jeopardize your trust in me. I'm telling you—the bag wasn't light. When I gave it to Easy, shit was straight."

"What's weird to me," Truck said, sitting back in his chair, "is how you immediately made this Easy's responsibility instead of saying you'll work with him to figure out the disconnect. You ain't hesitate to make it his problem."

"All due respect Truck, y'all ain't hesitating to make it *my* problem," Dave shrugged.

"Nigga, it's your problem! You run the corners, don't you?" Easy said, angry now. Romelo raised a hand, silencing the room.

"If you recall, I gave you 24 hours to figure the shit out. Now, I let you slide when you started having Calvin turn out pockets instead of doing it yourself. I let you delegate because I trust you and Malice to handle our corners. But it's clear either the workers are shorting Calvin, or he's shorting you. And please don't lie and say you counting after him because I know you're not. Make this right, Dave. And don't let it happen again," Romelo spat. Dave nodded, his eyes dropping to the floor. Romelo was angry. And he had a feeling this was bigger than some lost money.

"It won't, King. I'll figure it out," Dave promised.

"In the meantime, you need to come up off the shortfall," Truck said, lifting from the chair, a scowl on his face, "My cousin cares about your excuses, but I don't. It happened on your watch and involved people under your direction. You gotta make it right until you figure out which one of them niggas can't count. Easy and I will follow up."

"You're dismissed," Romelo said, waving Dave out of the room. Dave turned and left.

"What the fuck is going on? Last thing we need is new shit popping off," Easy grumbled, still upset. Romelo sighed. He didn't know. But he had a bad feeling it wasn't over.

Sadie

Sadie was behind the house practicing her shooting when Romelo came home. He didn't come to check on her, or even speak to her, so Sadie went to find him. She knew trying to sort out what was happening with Dave was wearing on him; she'd barely seen him in the last few days.

When Dave's deadline to find the culprit was up, he told Romelo he and Calvin traced it back to worker named Jamir, whose addict mother had been pinching off his supply for herself. Jamir was handled, but Romelo put some discreet eyes on Dave *and* Calvin after the incident; he was starting not to trust them anymore. But Sadie knew it was a hard stance for him to take, since Dave had been with him at the start of the organization, and he'd known the younger Calvin since he was practically a baby. Romelo's constant overthinking was triggering more headaches, and he wasn't sleeping. It didn't help that she couldn't put him to sleep because they weren't having sex.

Sadie found Romelo in his office, sitting in his chair, hands folded, elbows leaning on his desk. He looked bothered and Sadie knew he was worried he'd have to make a tough decision. He'd given her a ghost of a smile in greeting and said he wasn't hungry when she asked him about dinner. Sadie knew he needed to release whatever had him wound so tight, so she called Bianca. Her first thought was taking him out back to their shooting range to expel the extra energy, but then she thought of Bee—taking care of him was both of their jobs now, and this was a great way for all of them to spend some time relaxing.

"Are you done for the day?" Sadie asked Bianca, pacing back and forth in the family room as she talked on the phone.

"Yeah, I'm done. I need a bath and my weighted blanket; today was a mess."

"We have both of those here. You need to get here, Bee. Like, right now."

"Why? What's going on?"

"I don't know, but it's bad. Romelo came in, and didn't even want to eat. He's been holed up in his office, staring at the ceiling. It's not a migraine, I don't think. He's not in pain, he's... angry."

"Worrying someone you know, and trust is betraying you will weigh you down. I'll be right there," Bianca said and hung up the phone. Sadie went upstairs and started the tub, dumping aloe vera oil and rose oil. She set out towels and lit candles. Then she brought the whiskey decanter from the living room bar, a rocks glass, and a bucket of ice. By the time she was finished, Teddy was letting Bianca in the door. Sadie met her and they went into Romelo's office. He was sitting in his chair, hands still folded, staring at the empty far wall.

"Baby?" Sadie called him, keeping her voice soft. Romelo turned to them, a strained smile coming over his face. Sadie's heart broke. His head was hurting now; she could see it in his eyes.

"Hey, my beautiful babies. What's up?" he said.

"Come with us," Bianca said, holding out her hand.

"What's going on? Is something wrong?" he asked.

"Yes," Sadie replied, "With you. Come with us and unwind. You don't have to talk about it. But let us help you get the day off you." Romelo looked like he was going to protest, but they moved to his desk, pulling him up and taking him upstairs. In the bathroom, everyone stripped down and got into the warm water, Bianca against the wall of the tub, Romelo relaxing on her chest, and Sadie between his legs. She turned on the jets and the three of them sat there in the candlelight, enjoying the peace, and each other. Romelo sipped his drink, and slowly but surely, his shoulders relaxed. Neither Sadie nor Bianca asked him for details—they knew he wouldn't offer them even if they had.

Bianca rubbed Romelo's temples while Sadie massaged his hands and whispered how wonderful he was, and how much she loved him. She peered into the water, staring at the contrast of her lighter skin, against Romelo's orange-hued brown, and Bianca's deeper, darker brown. Sadie felt even more blessed they were all together.

"Thank you," Romelo's voice rumbled through the quiet, and his arms came around her belly, pulling her tighter against him as he relaxed further into Bee.

"Next time, don't sit with it so long. Let us make it better," Sadie whispered to him. He grunted what she assumed was an agreement.

"We'll make it a rule," Bianca chimed in, "All of us deal with things in our own way, and if we need alone time, we can have alone time. But when we need each other, we don't wait."

"I agree. We speak our needs, right away," Sadie said. Romelo sighed, and then all was quiet again.

"I need you tonight," his voice came softer, almost hesitantly, "I know we're waiting while we build our foundation. But I need to feel you, Shug. I need to feel you, Baby Girl. I've been wanting you both, and today—"

"You can have us, love," Bianca stopped him, her voice heavy with passion, "If it's what you need, you can have it." Sadie nodded in agreement. Romelo took care of them so well, hiding the world's ugliness from them. She knew what he did, and knew who he was, but it didn't erase him being her protector, and the man who loved her beyond measure. If this life couldn't change how she felt about her grandfather, father, and brothers, then it wouldn't change how she felt about Romelo.

Sadie sat up, moving to her knees and blowing out the candles around the tub. She moved them to the side, and then carefully rose to her feet, water dripping both from her body and the stray braids loose from her bun.

"Let's go to bed," she said. She got out of the tub, grabbing a towel and heading into the bedroom. Seconds later, she heard the splashes of water as her two lovers followed. Romelo pressed against her back, leaned down to kiss her neck. His hands came around to her breast and he squeezed the soft mounds as her nipples rose to his touch. Sadie moaned.

"It's been weeks, Shug. You're torturing me," he whispered between kisses.

"And me," Bianca said, stepping in front of her. Sadie gasped and Bianca swooped down, taking her mouth with insistence. Sadie whimpered, already drowning. She knew they packed a punch separately, but together? It was nearly too much. Bianca kissed her hard, her lips firm against Sadie's, her tongue seeking. Sadie pressed closer, moaned as Romelo's hands tugged her nipples and his mouth suctioned to her neck. She opened her mouth, wrapped her tongue around Bianca's, hummed as the nasty kiss made her blush to the tips of her hair.

"Ro, I need to taste her. I need her on my tongue," Bianca begged, sounding desperate. Romelo moaned and backed away, pulling her over to the bed. He bent at the knees and lifted Sadie onto the high bed, kissing her thighs as he laid her down. Bianca climbed on right after, and Sadie didn't even get to take a breath before the woman was turning her and spreading her thighs.

"Oh, you're still so pretty, Sadie," she whispered, staring in awe and lustful fascination. Sadie smiled bashfully, feeling warm, and getting impossibly wet. Romelo lay down next to her, grabbing her leg and holding it high as he maneuvered to catch her nipple with his tongue. Sadie moaned, and Bianca dropped, pushing Sadie's other thigh to widen them and licking her slit from top to bottom.

"Fuck!" Sadie cried out, trying to move away from the dual sensations. Romelo held her still, suckling at her breast as Bianca kissed her pussy, pushing her tongue inside to slurp her wetness.

"Taste fucking incredible..." Bianca whispered, using her fingers to part Sadie's pussy lips. Sadie whimpered as her clit was sucked softly. It was as good as she remembered. Bianca's mouth had always been one of her best assets. Sadie could feel herself charging toward an orgasm, and things were only getting started.

"Please..." she begged, almost overcome, "Oh my God!"

"You like Bee's mouth on your pussy, Shug? You like it?" Romelo whispered.

"Yes, oh yes. *Si, me gusta mucho* (Yes, I like it)," Sadie panted, her last words slipping into Spanish. Romelo laughed, and the rumble tickled her ears, tightened her nipples. How in the hell could a man's laugh turn her on so much?

"Bee looks so good eating you up. She looks like she's having a good time. I want to have a good time. Can I eat you too?" he went on, and Sadie's eyes rolled back in her head. She nodded, her breath coming in short bursts. Bianca moaned and smacked her lips as she licked Sadie's pussy over and over and sucked on her clit. Romelo played with her nipples, kissing her lips and neck, leaving her flushed and breathless. Bianca pushed two fingers into her, curling them and speeding up her tongue. Sadie's body bucked; she felt like she was on fire.

"I'm gonna cum—oh shit—Beeeeee," she called out, her legs splayed open, her wetness dripping, her pussy being gobbled, and her nipples being sucked and tugged. It wasn't enough, it was too much. Sadie screamed and her orgasm crested, slamming into her with force. Bianca moaned as she continued licking, and Romelo quickly moved behind her, lifting her hips and pushing inside of her.

"Ohhh shit!" Bianca wailed, lifting her head as she felt the intrusion. Romelo pushed her head down again.

"Keep eating. I didn't say stop. Take this dick," he ordered, and Bianca obeyed immediately, making Sadie even hotter as she watched her cool, calm, dancer girl melt like an ice cube for the King. Bianca's tongue moved over her, her lips sucked Sadie's juices as Romelo fucked her so hard, with a steady, pounding rhythm. He moaned with abandon as he thrust inside their girl, and Sadie could hear in his noises how much he'd missed being inside of her. It only made her hotter.

"Yes, yes. Fuck her harder. Bee, eat me faster. Oh shit!" Sadie grabbed her own nipples and her thighs shook. She was going to come again. Between the sight and the sensations, she was on the brink. Romelo groaned, his hips moving faster. His hands gripped Bianca's waist and pulled her to him, arching her more.

"Good ass pussy... missed this pussy. Gimme my pussy," Romelo mumbled as he pushed inside of Bianca. Sadie came with a gasp, her senses overwhelmed with everything she saw and felt. Her two loves were beautiful in the way they consumed one another, and her.

"Romelo, it's too much. Baby, it's too much," Bianca begged, lifting her head again. Sadie watched her come apart and it was one of the sexiest things she'd ever seen.

"It's not too much. It's made for you, like it's made for Shug. You got it, Baby Girl. You can take it," Romelo coaxed, fucking her harder. Bianca screamed and then muffled her sounds with a mouthful of Sadie's pussy. Sadie whimpered, her eyes widening. Bianca licked her, sucked her, whined into her pussy as Romelo pounded her. Sadie's thighs shook and her swollen clit was so sensitive it was almost aching.

"I'm coming... fuck, I'm coming again," she cried, her eyes closing. Bianca's hands gripped her thighs, and she exploded on Romelo's dick with a keening cry at the same moment Sadie's juices squirted, covering the bottom half of her face. Sadie moaned, tears leaking from her eyes. Her body shook and her orgasm blurred her vision. Bianca fell to the bed, rolling over and curling into a ball as she came hard. Romelo kissed her mouth, then moved up and slid inside of Sadie, turning her orgasm into multiples as he thrust twice before spilling inside her with a shout.

"Fuck!" he called out, pumping his hips. Sadie felt his warm release, whimpered as her pussy clenched around him. Her eyes closed.

"Sadie? Baby?" Bianca called. Sadie opened her eyes, blinking the room into focus. Bianca and Romelo were smiling at her, one wiping between her thighs with warm rag, and the other fixing a bonnet over her head.

"You two are incredible," she whispered, her throat slightly sore from screaming.

"You made us like this, Shug. Wanting you made us like this," Romelo said.

"You hungry, baby? We didn't have any dinner," Bianca said. Sadie nodded. Romelo got his cell phone and called downstairs to Scratch and Teddy. Thirty minutes later, they were all cuddled on the couch in the sitting area of the bedroom, with the TV on some random show. Sadie held a cheeseburger in one hand as she fed Romelo fries with the other. Romelo sat between her and Bianca, taking fries from Sadie's fingers with one bite and wolfing down a cheesesteak with the other. Bianca was on the other side, her feet in Romelo's lap as she tore through a Cobb salad with grilled chicken. She was scooping it with garlicky pita chips and Sadie smiled as she watched her girlfriend, sexually satisfied and well-fed, dancing as she ate, in her own personal heaven.

"Ain't shit changed," Romelo whispered with a smirk, "You make our girl come and give her some food and she's happier than a pig in mud." Sadie giggled, nodding.

"I can hear you," Bianca said, laughing, "Today was hectic. I needed this. And things clearly haven't changed with you, either. You're inhaling your sandwich like this is the first time you've eaten all day, which means it probably is. You've got to take better care of yourself, Ro."

"I do, baby. Today was hectic, like you said."

"He's gotten better with it," Sadie jumped in, "We've been trying to curb the onset of some of the migraines, and skipping meals can be a trigger, so I'm always on his nerves about it."

"You are, and in the best way," Romelo replied, finishing his sandwich, "Thank you, Shug." The three of them finished eating and watched more TV. Sadie was relaxed and content. Then, Romelo put her and Bianca in bed and picked up the phone to make some business calls. He checked in with Truck and Easy, then Scratch and Teddy. Lastly, he checked the cameras and made sure the house was locked down. Satisfied, he got into bed too.

"Lights down," he instructed, and their home system dimmed the lights. Bianca climbed over him and nudged him over, so he was between them. Sadie snuggled up to him, laying on his chest, and Bianca did the same on the other side.

"I can't go back to not feeling you," Sadie admitted on a sigh, "I know waiting was my idea, but I can't go back to not feeling you."

"No objections here," Romelo laughed, "I never liked the idea anyway."

"I understand what you wanted, and I can appreciate you making sure our foundation is strong. But I missed you both this way. So much," Bianca said.

"Not anymore," Sadie promised, closing her eyes and smiling when Romelo's lips pressed against her forehead, "You won't have to miss us anymore."

Five

Opening Night, no matter the show, is a whirlwind of noise and music, frazzled nerves and performance anxiety, makeup kits and sewing needles. Bianca went from dressing room to dressing room, checking off the performers, adjusting costumes, and calming pre-show jitters. Then she flitted around backstage, making sure everyone's marks were clear, and the lights and sound were ready to go. She wasn't in the first act, but she featured heavily in the second and third, so she wanted to do her part to organize before she had to clear her mind and focus on dancing. Bianca peeked out of the curtain at the audience, grinning when she spotted Romelo and Sadie in the front row. They were flanked by Keona and Nasima, with Bashir on Nasima's other side. Truck and Easy were working tonight.

"Bee, get ready. The second act will be here before you know it, and I am expecting you to shine," the director said, pulling her back from the curtain. Bianca turned to face him. Marcel wasn't the smiling type, but his eyes told her he was excited and proud. She nodded.

"I won't let you down, Marcel."

Marcel nodded and hurried away, calling for everyone to get in their places. The lights went down, and everyone went to their marks. The curtains opened and the classical chords of the performance began. Bianca watched the dancers for a few minutes, then went to her dressing room. She wiped herself down, refreshed her makeup, and smoothed her hair. Finally, she hydrated and stretched before getting into her costume. The music of the first act wound down, and there was thunderous applause from the audience. Bianca took a deep breath. Showtime.

Bianca took another bow, stepping forward for yet another curtain call. Camera flashes assaulted her vision, and the theater filled with applause, whistles, and foot stomps. She stepped back, finally ducking off to the side and hurrying to her dressing room. The other dancers offered her congratulations and expressed their satisfaction with the choreography and formations, both things she'd been a key part of. Bianca was proud of herself. She didn't miss the dance troupe at all, and she was back with Romelo and Sadie.

Once she was in her dressing room, Bianca sat down to rest. She wanted to wash her makeup off and put her sweats on, but there was still the after party and press pictures to deal with. Romelo offered to take everyone to dinner after she was done, but Bianca wanted a stiff drink, a big grilled chicken salad, and cuddles from her man, and woman. A knock at the door pulled her from her thoughts.

"Come in!" she yelled, grinning. She knew it was Sadie, coming to give her a congratulatory kiss.

The door opened. "Buttercup! You were wonderful!"

Bianca spun in her chair. "Tan? Charlie?" She stood up, her mouth open in shock. What were they doing here? Tanya Nance walked up, her smile bright. She and her husband hadn't changed—she was still short, plump and attractive with her tan skin and hazel eyes, and Charlie was a tall, husky, dark brown dreamboat. They were the same, but Bianca... wasn't.

"Hi Bee. Aren't you glad to see us?"

"I—I don't—what are you doing here?"

"We weren't going to miss your first show as Artist-In-Residence," Charlie said, coming up to her. He handed her a bouquet of perfect, pink, roses. Bianca lowered her nose to them, humming at their fragrance. She looked up again. Charlie and Tanya were still the same—warm, welcoming, with arms open for her like she'd never left them. Bianca wouldn't pretend she didn't appreciate their gesture but seeing them again wasn't something she ever thought would happen. She hadn't even reached out to them in the weeks she'd been home.

"I can't believe this," she finally spoke, "I can't believe you came all this way for me."

"We show up for the people we care about," Tanya said, "We know how important this is for your career. Of course, we're going to be here for you. And why so shy, Buttercup? Can't we even get a hug?"

"I—I mean—of c-course." Bianca was confused. They flew all the way across the country for her? She'd made it very clear when she left them, she wasn't looking to maintain the relationship because she was hoping to win Romelo and Sadie back. They could have sent a card or called to wish her good luck. What did it mean that they'd flown all the way here? She put the flowers down on her chair. Bianca leaned forward and hugged Charlie first, keeping it short and making sure she didn't rub up against him. When she got to Tanya, the woman hugged her so tightly, Bianca thought she'd lose circulation. Tanya leaned up after, pressing her lips to Bianca's. Bianca squeaked in surprise and pulled away.

"The one night Romelo convinces me to leave my gun at home, bitches wanna try me. Why are your lips on my girlfriend?" Sadie said, as she and Romelo walked in. Bianca shook her head, and stepped further away from Tanya, ignoring the hurt in her eyes.

Tanya turned, silenced by the look on Sadie's face. She leaned closer to Charlie, looking to Bianca for help. Bianca was angry and flustered. She obviously couldn't let Sadie hurt Tanya, but she couldn't defend Tanya's actions without hurting Sadie.

"Ro, Sadie, this is Tanya and Charlie Nance. Y-you remember I told you about them," Bianca mumbled. No one moved to shake hands or even wave.

"I remember you telling us they lived on the other side of the country," Romelo said, his voice soft, but lethal. He was carrying a big bouquet of purple tulips to match her hair and Bianca wanted to cry. They were finally learning to trust her again. Tanya and Charlie were going to undo weeks of headway she was making with her lovers.

"We um—we wanted to come and support Buttercup at her first show," Charlie said, getting a little more bass in his voice. Bianca stared helplessly. Romelo wasn't the person you wanted to poke your chest out at. Romelo stared at Charlie, then he laughed, but it had no humor.

"I know you want to look tough in front of your wife, but I ain't the nigga to do it with. And kill the nickname shit. She ain't your Buttercup no more, and I was under the impression she made that clear to you. Baby Girl, did you invite them here?"

"No, Romelo, of course not. I haven't even spoken to them since... I wouldn't do that. Please believe me," she pleaded, focusing on him and Sadie. She reached for her girlfriend's hand, willing her to reach back. Sadie's fingers wrapped around hers and Bianca finally felt like she could breathe.

"You came here uninvited and put your lips where they don't belong. Am I understanding this correctly?" Sadie said, addressing Tanya again. Tanya, to her credit, didn't flinch.

"Butter—Bianca said there was a chance she'd ruined things beyond repair, and you wouldn't want her back. We were hoping—we thought maybe—"

"You flew here on the chance they rejected me, without hearing from me, or even reaching out? Why would you do something like this?" Bianca demanded of Tanya. Charlie looked embarrassed and she knew most of this was his wife's doing, and he was indulging her, as he usually did.

"They don't deserve you, Buttercup! Charlie and I were the ones who picked up your pieces when they left you brokenhearted—"

"I left them! I explained what happened. Tanya, you have no right. Romelo and Sadie were everything to me then. They're everything to me now. You shouldn't have done this," Bianca said, feeling awful inside. The last thing she wanted was to hurt someone who'd been so good to her. But she couldn't fuck up what she had a second time. She wouldn't.

"You said you were in two separate relationships. Do you really want to be with people who have you torn? Juggling your time, while they ration theirs?" Charlie finally spoke again. Romelo growled, and his fists clenched.

"I gave you fair warning I wasn't the nigga to grandstand with," he said, putting Bianca's flowers down so he could stand face to face with Charlie, "Listen closely, cause I don't repeat myself: there is nothing you have ever given my woman she wasn't getting from me, and Sadie. You and your wife were the stand-ins for what Bianca really wanted. You couldn't match me on your best day—not in heart size, not in dick size, and especially not in wallet size. Whatever you were hoping to prove by coming here, you didn't. And your pride gon get your fucking chest caved in. I suggest you see if you can get an earlier flight home."

Bianca shivered after Romelo finished speaking, feeling his rage all over her. He didn't like being tested.

Charlie swallowed, the fear in his eyes obvious, "A-are y-you threatening us?"

Romelo laughed. "I'm the King, nigga. I don't threaten—I decree. I command, and my orders are carried out. Don't make me have to use one of my orders to carry you out."

Tanya wrapped her arms around her husband. "Bianca, are you going to let him speak to us like this?"

"What else is she supposed to do? She didn't ask you to assume she was missing you, or come here, or kiss her. You and your husband have overstepped your boundaries. This being my woman's place of business is the only reason I haven't overstepped mine. Y'all need to leave," Sadie said, holding onto Bianca tighter.

Bianca was sad. It should never have had to come to this. Her big night was pretty much ruined now. Tanya and Charlie weren't as cool as she thought, and now Romelo and Sadie may be angry with her too. They were defending her now, but she knew part of them wondered if she'd been leading Tanya and Charlie on in some way, keeping them in the wings as a back-up plan. She didn't know how to prove to them she didn't want anyone else, but she had to try.

"Tan, Charlie, I appreciate you coming all this way. But I didn't ask you to. You shouldn't have assumed the state of my relationship with Romelo and Sadie, and you shouldn't have used half-truths to question their love for me. I'm sorry this didn't turn out like you thought. But I'm happy now, and I have everything I want. I would've told you if you'd only asked."

"This is who you want to be with? We didn't mean anything to you?" Tanya kept going, tears on her cheeks. Bianca was sure she was going to be sick. This was turning into a soap opera right before her eyes, and she was the main character.

"This is who I *am* with," she replied to Tanya, her voice stronger, "You did mean something to me Tan, which is why I was hoping we'd still be friends. But I made it clear who I loved. It's not my fault you chose not to hear me."

"My woman had a great performance and you two have ruined her mood when she still needs to go smile and take pictures at this after party. I know she wants to get off her feet and out of her makeup and curl up in my arms and now she can't. She's tired because of y'all and now she has to go pretend she's not. It's time to go," Romelo said, and like magic, Scratch and Teddy appeared at the door to her dressing room.

"Can you find the door? If not, my associates can show you where it is," he continued. Charlie took one look at Scratch and Teddy and nodded his head.

"We can find it," he mumbled and dragged a crying Tanya from the room. Bianca wanted to cry herself. Romelo was 100% correct. The last thing she wanted to do was smile and take pictures with the cast and crew at some after party. But she would. Because she loved this job already, and she wouldn't jeopardize it.

"Come on, baby. Let's get you a drink," Sadie soothed her. Bianca held tight to Sadie and picked up her purple flowers with the other hand. They left the dressing room with Romelo bringing up the rear. She had her loves, and soon there would be drinks. Maybe tonight could be salvaged after all.

<u>Romelo</u>

Romelo lifted Bianca's thigh, opening her legs wide and sliding into her pussy from behind. Bianca whimpered, her wetness easing the way. She melted around him, holding him snugly within her tight walls. Romelo sighed and started to move, fucking her with long, deep, strokes. He must have done something good in a previous life to be blessed with two women who felt completely like home. He was never pulling out of either one of them again.

"He better than me, Baby Girl? Charlie fuck you good like this?" Romelo whispered in his girlfriend's ear.

"No, King. No one's better than you. Nobody fucks me good like you."

"That's what the fuck I thought," he boasted, filling her again and again. Bianca cried out, moving her ass against him, taking him, gripping him. Romelo kissed her neck, sucking on the soft flesh and making sure he left his mark. They moved together, their sex sounds filling up the room, their chemistry as strong as ever.

Romelo growled, unable to hold back how good it felt to be inside Bianca again. Her desperate moans filled him up, stroked his ego. He was drowning in her wetness, fully under her spell, and he didn't want to ever lose her again. The only thing missing was the sweet taste of Sadie on his tongue while he fucked their dancer girl. *But no worries*, he thought, *when she comes to spend the night, we're turning her every way but loose.*

"Ro, I'm coming!" Bianca yelled.

"Come on then, Baby Girl. You been so good; this pussy so good. You deserve to come, don't you? Don't you, Baby Girl?"

"Yessssss," Bianca wailed. He pushed into her, thrusting hard, still holding her leg up so she'd get every inch of him. Bianca gasped, then moaned loudly, her orgasm crashing into her. Her pussy clamped around him, her wetness leaked from her. Romelo couldn't help himself. He groaned, spilling inside her, coming so hard he had to close his eyes. Bianca was shaking, soft whimpers coming from her mouth. Romelo pulled out, letting her leg down gently. Bianca immediately turned into his arms. She kissed his neck.

"I'm gonna be late for rehearsal," she said with a soft chuckle. Romelo laughed too. He was about to be late for a meeting himself. He stopped by Bianca's place to give her something—a necklace she'd lost when she walked out the year before. He found it on the floor in the corner of his closet not long after she left. Romelo knew she hadn't intended to leave it. Bianca was adopted as a toddler, and the necklace was all she had of her birth mother. When he presented it to her, she cried, saying she'd spent the entire first month away from them crying herself to sleep because she thought it was lost forever. Her gratitude and joy at being reunited with something she didn't think she'd ever see again led to kisses, and then more.

Things had been quiet on the relationship front since the night Tanya and Charlie crashed the first performance. Romelo and Sadie plied Bianca with drinks and support while she showed her face at the after party, then they all went to the house for a bubble bath and relaxation. Bianca explained again how Tanya and Charlie made assumptions, and she never led them on. Romelo believed her; she looked entirely too shell-shocked by their appearance to have invited them. Bee gave them her body until it was sore, telling them how much she loved them. They ended the night with more drinks, pizza, wings and Bee's usual grilled chicken salad.

Romelo was annoyed he'd had to almost get into "King" mode on Tanya and Charlie, but it was clear it wasn't Bianca's fault, and he remembered Easy's words about not tripping her up with the past. They were moving forward, all three of them.

"Let me get up. I have a meeting," he finally said, lifting himself from the bed. He went into the bathroom and turned on the shower, knowing Bee would join him. They washed quickly and

Romelo dressed in his joggers and t-shirt while Bianca got into her leotards and tights. He walked her to the rehearsal space and kissed her goodbye before heading to the warehouse.

Things were also quiet on the organizational front, but not the kind of quiet Romelo liked. There hadn't been any more shortages in money, but Dave was still moving funny, showing up late to meetings, shifting corner boys and giving them new blocks. He said they were getting too complacent, and he was trying to weed out anymore thieves by shaking things up, but Romelo was having a hard time believing him. Easy, ever the watcher, was observing everything and taking notes, but Dave had been a part of the organization for years, and no one wanted to move until they were sure he was on some bullshit.

Teddy pulled up to the back entrance of the warehouse and let Romelo out of the car. Scratch was already there; he'd been tasked with watching over Sadie while she was home, but she'd gone shopping with Nas, Key, and little EJ and Truck had Nas's security watching all of them. Romelo entered the warehouse, passing the open area and heading up the stairs to the office. Easy and Truck were there, along with Keys, who was tapping away on his laptop, as usual.

"Sup?" he greeted everyone, and they nodded their heads in return. Romelo sat behind the desk in the room, sighing. Memories of Bianca's sweet smell, and her soft skin, floated through his mind. He could have lain up with her all day.

"Keys, what you got for us?" he started the meeting. He needed to get this information out of the way, so he could dismiss the hacker and have a private meeting with his Number Two and Three.

Langston Jones looked up with a grimace. "The house turned out to be a bit more layered than I thought. I assumed it was property of the city, but it's not. And I had to cut through like ten layers of red tape to find out who owned it. But it belongs to someone name Etta Burns."

"Who is she?" Easy asked.

Keys pushed his glasses up on his nose. "Someone I haven't been able to find. According to records, she's 85 years old. I can't find a soul who's seen her in the last ten years. But she somehow signed the rental agreement for the house across the street from our trap."

"Strange. Because why is the owner's information buried? Who is she that someone would need to hide it?" Truck said, his forehead creased in confusion.

"What's even more strange, is the person who rented the house hasn't been seen since they moved in. The U-Haul Easy caught was the one and only sign of life," Keys finished.

Romelo scowled. "Sounds like surveillance to me. Has Dave said anything about the house?"

"He said we were being paranoid, and it was a regular couple with kids. Swears he's seen them, but no one else has," Keys said, going back to typing on his laptop.

"He's still lying, Melo," Truck said, cracking his knuckles, "I don't like being lied to."

"Neither do I, cuz. But if we exposed him now, we won't find out who's watching us, or what they want. We gotta give him a little more rope. He'll hang himself soon. He's already slipping, giving us light bags, and moving corner boys around."

"You think he's on that shit?" Easy jumped in. "He could be pinching off product for himself. Maybe he thought Jamir was about to give him away. It's bad enough he and Calvin 'handled' it without giving me and Truck a heads up."

"But we did send the cleanup crew after he told us," Truck said, pulling out his phone, "I'm gonna see what they know."

"In the meantime, Keys, see if you can find any camera feeds close by we can hack into. Thanks, my man. Perfect, as always," Romelo said. Keys closed his laptop and stood up, dapping them all up before leaving the room. Easy locked the door behind him.

"We need a fake out at the trap in Dave's territory; go to the back-up," Romelo decreed. A fake out was a staged robbery and shut down of a location in their network. Whenever they suspected a location was compromised, Romelo used their enforcers to pretend to jack it and then burn it out, to get the product moved. Enemies would think they'd been hit, assume the King had a weakness, and was scrambling, which would make them relax and help expose them.

Romelo, Truck, and Easy kept talking, brainstorming, and putting safeguards in place. Taking Dave wouldn't be any good if they couldn't figure out his end game, and whether anyone else was involved.

"Anything else y'all wanna talk about?" Romelo said, a few hours later. He was anxious to get home. Sadie would be there, and he wanted to eat dinner and relax with her.

Truck sighed. "Nas is pregnant."

Romelo smiled. He knew it was only a matter of time. Nasima coming home was the completion of Trevino and Bashir, and he figured they wouldn't hesitate to cement their home and family.

"Congratulations, cuz," he said, meaning it. Truck smiled. Romelo was so proud of his cousin. He'd made it, with all the odds stacked against him, and he'd found not one, but two people to love him and make a home with him.

"Yeah, we're nearly out of the first trimester, so Nas says I can tell the fam now. The only thing is, I planned to back away from the organization before she started having babies. Obviously, I can't now. And truth be told, it don't feel right. I mean... for years

I saw myself as a machine, a soldier in your army, Melo. I didn't want to hear what you were telling me about this organization being mine too. But this shit with Dave is making me look at things differently. We've been the family a lot of these niggas never had, Dave included. I got into this to be with you and protect you. If someone is turning their back on our family and coming for your head, they're coming for mine too," Truck said.

"And we're gonna snuff them out, I promise you," Romelo said, his voice hard, "I understand your worry, and I know this is a delicate time for Nas. We'll handle this shit with Dave, and then we can sit down with our most loyal and figure out how we *all* can move differently. We spend more time on our illegal dealings, but we have more clean money than we know what to do with, also. Maybe it's time to calm down. Easy and Keona have a kid too, and I know he's been having some of the same thoughts."

"Two kids," Easy mumbled, biting back a grin.

"What did you say?" Truck asked.

Easy looked up at them, smiling. "I said two kids. Key's pregnant too."

"Damn, you niggas don't waste no time, do you?" Romelo laughed.

"Hell naw. Last time, I missed everything with Key and EJ. I wanna be there for every milestone this time," Easy said.

"You know how long I waited for Nas to come home? I ain't never coming up off her. And you already know Butta is obsessed with her. Shit, if I wasn't obsessed with both of them, I'd be jealous."

Romelo laughed at his cousin. "I know how you feel. Speaking of, let me get my ass home."

Sadie

Sadie spent the day practicing her shooting, researching buyers for their newest shipment of weapons, and then shopping with Nas, Keona, and EJ. Nasima announced her pregnancy to them, only for Keona to turn around and do the same thing. Their shopping trip turned into a celebration and Sadie was excited to be an auntie again. EJ was her heart, and she couldn't wait for more babies. It got her thinking of her own womb. She and Romelo talked about becoming parents, and even though they hadn't landed on any firm plans for pregnancy, she wasn't on anything to prevent it. And now she wondered what it would be like to carry Romelo's baby. Bianca made it clear her dancing career would be her only baby for a while longer, but Sadie was ready.

"Shug! I'm home, baby!" Romelo said, coming into the kitchen. Sadie was plating their dinner—lemon and herb roast chicken with garlic green beans and roasted potatoes. She looked up when he entered the room, smiling at his handsome face. Romelo grinned back, coming to the island to kiss her forehead, then her lips.

"Hey love," she spoke to him. He moved behind her, grabbing two glasses and pouring them both wine. He took it to the table and came back for the plates while Sadie made sure everything was off, and the extra food was covered. Then she sat down with her love and bowed her head so he could pray over their food.

"Everything go okay today?" she asked. Romelo nodded.

"We ironed some details and put some things in place. Keys came by and gave us an update. We only need a little more intel. On a brighter note, I'm assuming Nas and Keona told you what Truck and Easy told me?"

"Yeah," Sadie replied with a grin, "Isn't it exciting? I told the girls I would help them both decorate the babies' rooms and plan the showers."

"What did they say?"

"They were happy I could take time out of my busy schedule of shooting things to help," Sadie laughed. Romelo laughed with her.

"You think we might be ready for a baby?" she continued, trying to see Romelo's reaction to the topic. Her man smiled a soft smile and reached for her hand.

"I'm ready whenever you are, Shug," he said, "and this conversation is coming at a good time. I've been doing some thinking about us being more lowkey and trying to figure out where we can pull back. Maybe I can stick with product and get out of the weapons business, you know? It would free us both up and cut back on Truck's security detail work. We have enough legitimate business; we certainly won't need the money."

"Wow." Sadie was happy he was ready to consider parenthood with her, but changing the business was a surprise she wasn't expecting. The weapons were her main job. What would happen if the organization didn't need her anymore? Sadie wanted to be a mother, but she didn't think she'd have to give up her work.

"Is 'wow' all you have to say?" Romelo asked.

"You're folding up half the business? When did you decide that?"

"I haven't decided anything, Shug. It was a suggestion. If we're going to be starting families, we need a way to refocus and keep things calmer. The product was our first business; weapons was something we added later, so moving on from it should be easier. And it's not half the business, not even close. Which is the other reason I suggested it."

"Oh," she said, "What will *I* do if you pull back from the weapons?"

Romelo chuckled. "Whatever you want to, Shug. One of our legit businesses is a gun shop. Hell, I'll buy you a gun range. You can teach other women to protect themselves, make them as good as you."

Sadie brightened. She hadn't thought of that. "You'd really do it for me, wouldn't you?"

"Tomorrow, if you tell me to. Sadie, I will do anything to make you happy."

"I know. But I love it when you remind me." The two of them went back to eating.

"Hey," Romelo said, putting his fork down, "I'm serious. I don't like you thinking I would leave you hanging if we refocused the business. There's always a place for you here. You hear me, Sadie Marie?"

"I hear you, baby. I promise, I hear you. Sometimes my insecurities get the best of me."

"What are you insecure about?"

"I mean... you're the King. Bee is a well-known dancer. You both have a thing—your *own* thing. I don't have anything that's mine, except what's probably an unhealthy knowledge of weaponry," Sadie said with a giggle.

Romeo smirked. "Your mind and your trigger finger are two of my favorite things about you. But like I said, if you want to stay with guns, we have ways you can do it, no matter what happens with the business. I will show up for you in whatever way you need. You have my heart, and my back, and there's always a place for you beside me."

When he finished speaking, Sadie sat there, her eyes full of happy tears. She loved it when Romelo reassured her.

"Finish your food so I can ravage you, old man," she said.

"I got your old man," Romelo laughed and picked up his fork again.

Later in bed, Sadie straddled Romelo, her body warm and flushed, her pussy wet and ready for him. She shifted up and forward so he could slide inside. The moment he filled her up, Sadie moaned. He felt so good, so right. He was perfect inside of her. She started to move. His hands came up, holding her waist, rubbing down to her thighs. Sadie sighed. She loved Romelo's hands on her. She loved it even more when he turned her bottom red with his heavy hands.

Impact play was something relatively new for the couple. Sadie discovering she enjoyed being spanked was purely accidental, but once the two of them talked about boundaries, it became something they both looked forward to. They even had a drawer of assorted paddles and floggers they used when they were feeling adventurous. But on quiet nights at home like this one, Romelo's big hands would more than do.

"What were you saying? I'm an old man?" Romelo teased, lifting his hips and pushing deeper.

Sadie whimpered. "I thought—I didn't know if—"

A sharp smack stung her as Romelo's hand connected with her ass. "You thought what?"

Sadie cried out, the pleasure/ pain making her wetter. *He makes it hurt so good*, Sadie thought, riding him faster. She loved when he was forceful, and Sadie dug her nails into his chest, knowing the sting would make him punish her more. Romelo didn't disappoint, spanking her again and again, as she moved her hips, her wet pussy swallowing his dick over and over.

"You better answer me," he growled, spanking her again. Sadie came, her pussy leaking on him.

"Oh fuck! Baby I—y-you smelled like Bee's soap when you came in. I knew you'd b-been with her and I didn't know if you'd h-have the energy for m-me," she wailed. Romelo smacked her bottom, and she fluttered around him, clamping his dick. He moaned loudly.

"I always have enough energy to satisfy you," he bit out, his eyes closing. Sadie rode him faster still, her pussy soaking wet from the spanking he'd given her. They came together, and as Romelo shot his warm release into her gushy walls, Sadie prayed for her man's peace. She prayed he'd have the discernment to weed out the snakes. And she prayed he would give them a child.

Afterward, she snuggled close to Romelo, soothed by his heartbeat in her ear. She loved this man so completely. He and Bianca rescued her from a dating pool where she was constantly told she was too loud, too fat, too much, and not feminine enough. And now she had two perfect lovers, for whom she'd bust as many guns and have as many babies as she could.

Six

S"Could the dress get any shorter? If you bend over, everyone will see your damn hooha," Sadie complained as they got into the car. Bianca laughed.

"You sound like Romelo right now."

"And you sound like you don't care enough about our pussy being on display. I'm with Romelo on this," Sadie grumbled. Bianca moved closer to Sadie on the backseat, leaning down to kiss her in the center of her bouncy cleavage. Sadie sighed with pleasure, her light skin flushing pink where Bianca's lips were.

"I'm not the only one who looks good enough to eat tonight, Sadie," she whispered. Sadie smiled and turned away from the heat in Bianca's gaze. Bianca giggled and leaned up. The car pulled off and they sat back to enjoy the ride.

The two women were meeting Nas and Keona at a nightclub called Sparkle City, one of the many legitimate businesses owned by King Davis's organization. They were celebrating the new babies with a night in VIP, plus Sadie pointed out they hadn't had a girl's night since everyone came back home. Nasima and Keona were only too happy to get outside before they were so far along it was too hard. The guys recommended Sparkle City because it would be easy to secure and monitor them; Romelo made sure they had a private section and their own bottle girl.

Sparkle City was an indulgent, adult playground, with exotic dancers, a stage area for performances, and a more intimate lounge on the second floor. Scratch picked up Nasima and Keona before heading to the club and dropping the women off in front. The bouncer opened the door and he and Scratch ushered them in. Scratch met up with Nasima's guard, a guy only known as Bully, and they escorted the women to VIP. Bully stood guard at the entrance to the section while everyone got comfortable. Sadie smiled, feeling good about the night—and knowing she looked good as well. She smoothed her hands over her new knotless braids. She was wearing a black mini skirt and crop top set, her thighs, shoulders, and belly exposed. Sadie finished her outfit with low-heeled black booties, and diamonds on her ears and wrist. Bianca wore a silver metallic bandage dress that stopped above her knees and silver stiletto heels. Her purple hair was pinned up and she wore dangling diamond earrings in her ears—a gift from Romelo.

"This is going to be so much fun!" Nasima said over the music as she danced in her seat. Both her and Keona opted to wear rompers to be dressy and comfortable. Nasima's was red, and strapless, and she wore matching red wedge sneakers and gold jewelry. Keona's romper was a halter in hunter green, and she wore gold flats and gold jewelry.

"Got some drinks for y'all," a pretty woman with red hair entered the section, tray in hand. She was wearing the standard sparkly bandeau top and black high waisted shorts required of the bottle girls of the club, "My name is Jules, and I will be serving you guys all night. I have four peach pina coladas, two virgins. I'll be right back with some water." Jules smiled at them and sat the tray down. The women spoke back and gathered around, toasting the night and each other. Jules came right back with the bottled water in a bucket of ice and four cups.

"Thank you, Jules," Sadie said, reaching into her cleavage for some cash to tip.

Jules waved her away with a wink. "Put your money away. King already took care of me. Truth be told, I'm honored he trusts me to take care of his girls."

Bianca grinned. Sadie laughed at her obvious joy. The only thing her dancer girl loved more than her pointe shoes was being Romelo's Baby Girl. And Sadie understood. His love was like sunshine. The women settled in for a good night, dancing in their section, laughing at themselves and people watching. They felt safe and protected.

"Are y'all ready for a special treat?" The DJ stopped the music and spoke into the mic, "After years on hiatus, he's finally making his way back on the music scene—give it up for Aaron Mathis!"

The women yelled with excitement and stood up, carrying their drinks over to the railing as Aaron Mathis hit the stage. Aaron was a major R&B star who left the spotlight suddenly after his long-time girlfriend/ manager dumped him. Rumor had it, after years of infidelity, she snapped, and his guilty heart wouldn't let him make new music without her. No one had seen him in years. Sadie was so hype. How did Romelo manage to get a reclusive former R&B star out of hiding to do a show?

"Oh, my goodness. I LOVE Aaron Mathis! How in the hell did Romelo pull this off?" Keona said. Aaron strummed his guitar and the crowd went crazy. For the next hour, he played all his older hits while Sadie and her girls danced and sang lyrics to one another and took every drink Jules brought up to them.

Once Aaron left the stage, the DJ went back to spinning and the women sat down.

"This is so much fun. We have to make it a point to hang out, at least twice a month. Brunch, mani/pedis, whatever," Nasima said, pulling two pins from her cleavage and swooping her long hair into an updo.

"I agree. I love shit like this," Bianca said, more than a little tipsy.

"As long as we can get tacos after. All this dancing has me and baby hungry," Keona said. They all burst into laughter. Sadie turned her head, looking around the crowded club. In the corner, she saw two men arguing. It looked like one of the men was Calvin. Their exchange looked hostile, and they pushed each other before the other man walked off. Calvin went in the other direction, blending into the crowd. And Sadie had a bad feeling. The feeling was solidified when she saw another guy meet up with the first guy and then they both followed Calvin. Sadie pulled out her phone and texted Scratch to come and get them.

"We need to get ready to go," she said to the others, trying to stay calm. They all turned to her, staring curiously, but no one questioned it. Everyone gathered their things.

"Bully, can you take us to the car? We're ready," Nasima called out to him. He held up one finger for her to wait and pulled out his cell phone. Nasima pulled hers out too and Sadie knew she was texting Truck. Keona followed suit, and Sadie opened her phone to text Romelo. She bent down to get Bianca's clutch off the floor and the gunshots rang out. Everyone screamed, and it was like a stampede as people tried to get out of the club. Sadie dropped to the floor and pulled Bianca down with her, yelling at Nas and Key to get down. She heard glass breaking and felt the floor moving as people ran out.

"Sadie! Come on, baby," Romelo pulled her up and handed her to Scratch before grabbing Bianca. Bashir was practically carrying Nasima and Easy had Keona wrapped in his arms. The guys led them out of the section to the main floor and out the back entrance. Moments later, they were in two cars and driving into the night. Sadie was shaking with relief, and didn't even realize there were tears on her cheeks.

"I got you, Shug. I got both of you. I'm here, baby," Romelo soothed, rocking them both in his arms. Sadie reached for Bianca's hand and the two of them held tight to their King.

When they got home, Romelo fed them, bathed them, and rubbed them down. He laid with them until they were asleep in his arms. The last thing Sadie remembered before sleep took her was the gentle press of Romelo's lips on hers, and his whispered promise that someone was going to pay.

Romelo

Romelo considered himself mostly a peaceful man. Slow to anger, not prone to excessive violence. But tonight, he wanted blood. Someone had gotten into his club with a gun. They could have shot his babies. They could have taken his heart. They were going to feel the wrath of the King.

Scratch, who was on duty with Bully, watching the girls discreetly, saw Calvin disappear into the crowd and caught a flash of the metal from his gun. He texted Romelo, who called in Truck to scoop Calvin up and figure out why he was in their very legal establishment with an illegal weapon. The workers weren't allowed to cross those lines. If they were patrons, they had to behave as such, and they weren't permitted to conduct business at Sparkle City. Romelo texted Scratch to get the girls out, not knowing Sadie had peeped and was doing the same thing. In the next moment, he, Easy and Truck got a text from Bully, and then their women, respectively. He was coming in the back door with Easy and Bash when the shots rang out. His only priority _then_ was getting his family to safety. But _now_? Now, he wanted blood.

"Anybody talking yet?" Romelo asked, walking into the room. They were in the basement of a laundromat he owned, behind an iron door with a keypad lock. He and Teddy entered the main area (Scratch was at home with Bee and Sadie) and looked around. It was an open space, with hooks attached to the ceiling and all kinds of weaponry on the walls. Four men were hanging from the hooks with rope—Calvin, the two men who'd followed him into the club, and Lou, the bouncer who was on door duty. Truck and Easy stood off to the side, and Dave was sitting backwards in a chair, looking nonchalant. Truck called him because Calvin was his man. His worker, his problem too.

"Yeah, Lou's been talking. But he didn't have much," Truck said. Romelo walked up to one of the men. Lou was the bouncer at the door tonight, the one who for a price, let Calvin in without patting him down. Lou hung his head in shame, his breaths shallow and quick, like he couldn't catch his breath. Romelo stared at him, his heart black with rage. He pulled his gun before anyone could blink and shot Lou in the head. Dave and Calvin jumped. Truck and Easy shrugged.

"Fuck him," Romelo spat, "There's no excuse he could give me to justify putting my family in danger. What about you, Calvin? You got anything to say to me? Lou let you in, and then you vouched for these niggas? Is that what happened?"

Calvin stayed silent, his face hard. He glanced over at Dave, as if he expected him to come to his aid. Dave looked away, his eyes focused on the wall of weapons.

"Gotta admire a man who has a code. I don't give a fuck though," Truck said, walking over. He swung the spiked bat in his hands, hitting one of the other men in the solar plexus. His screams echoed through the room, and Calvin looked scared. Truck wasn't only a sniper, and expert marksman, putting men out of their misery with speed and accuracy. He was also a weapons aficionado, hand to hand specialist, and bare-knuckle brawler who could kill you slow... and make it hurt.

"Now," Truck continued leaning closer to the man he'd hit, "Why were you and your friend in our club with guns?"

"Calvin said he needed our help with a rip. He wanted to empty the safe without it tracing back to him. He gave us the safe combination and access to the office. He was supposed to bust his gun in the air after we were done, cause enough chaos so we could sneak out in the panic. At the last minute, he chickened out, and said he didn't want to do it. Nigga refused to pay us, so—"

"So y'all tried to have a real shootout in my gotdamn club," Romelo interrupted. He raised his gun and fired at the man who spoke, hitting him in the throat. Blood splattered on both Calvin and his friend, and the friend started to cry. Romelo was hot, blood rushing through his veins, his head starting to pound. He was overextending himself—he needed to go home, let Truck and Easy handle the rest. But he couldn't. These three scared his girls, jammed up his business, tried to steal his money. Something bigger was at play, and he needed to find out what it was. Someone was coming for his crown, and that someone had a hard lesson to learn.

"You good, King?" Easy asked. Romelo nodded.

Easy pushed off the wall and came forward. He went to the other attempted robber, pulling a hunting knife from his pants. He unsheathed the knife and jammed it into the man's thigh, twisting it. The man screamed, and Calvin turned away, a look of angry resignation on his face.

"I think I might have nicked your femoral artery. You might want to tell me where you and your boy came from before you bleed out. We found a crayon on the floor of the car y'all came in. My guess is, you got a kid at home you color with. I know this, because I do too. If I have to find out who you are myself, your family will suffer," Easy spoke in a calm voice, using the man's shirt to wipe the blood from his knife.

"W-we came from a few hours away. We used to work f-for the Wolf. Calvin said this was a good way to get some payback and some money. Work's been slow since y'all blew up our operation," the man blubbered. Easy nodded, satisfied.

"Shut the fuck up!" Calvin screamed, pulling against his bonds, his body flopping around like a fish.

Truck laughed. "You probably didn't have time to develop any real loyalty, but you needed to at least make sure they don't crack under pressure, my nigga. Damn."

"Truck told me I should have killed everyone at the compound that day. Here I go trying to give niggas a chance," Romelo grumbled, angry with himself now too, "Dave, you're up." He finally turned to look at his lieutenant. Dave stared at them, looking shell-shocked and disturbed. Romelo shook his head.

After the fake out and the set up in the new trap, things calmed down a little. Keys reported the house across the way was randomly boarded up, like no one had ever moved in, which confirmed Romelo's suspicion that it was an attempt at surveillance. And now he had Truck and Easy doing pop-ups on Dave at the new trap, counting after Calvin and sometimes turning out pockets themselves. Dave was resentful of being babysat, but he knew better than to complain about it.

"Umm... what you need me to do, King?" he said, standing up and walking over. Romelo noticed how he refused to look Calvin in the eye, and he didn't appear angry or disappointed with him. *He looks like he feels sorry for him,* Romelo thought, *like he can get him out of this, but he won't.*

"Calvin tried to rob me, which means he betrayed us, and you. He's your protege. Don't you care about him turning against us? Aren't you worried about other ways he may have double-crossed you?"

"He's never done anything like this as far as I know, King," Dave said, swallowing hard.

"You had him turning out pockets and counting our money. I know you feel some type of way," Truck pressed. He picked up his bat, going over to Calvin and looking at him with mayhem in his eyes. Romelo blinked, trying to ward off the aching in his head. He wanted Dave to step up, so this had a chance of being quick. If he let Truck loose, they might be here for hours.

"He wasn't short. I-I never cared about his friends or anything. I don't even know how he found these niggas," Dave insisted, but he still wouldn't look Calvin in the eye.

"Keys should have that information by morning. You got anything to say, Calvin? Wanna tell us how you got office access in the first place? No?" Easy asked. Calvin balled his face up, but he refused to talk. Romelo admired his attitude.

"You're good, Calvin. Don't even worry about it. We already know our club manager is harboring a little crush on you, hoping you'll leave your girlfriend for her. You probably stole and copied Macy's keys and codes. Or maybe you got them directly from her. We should bring Macy in here too, huh?" Easy continued. In his incessant watching, Easy peeped Calvin meeting up with Macy, and their head bottle girl Jules confirmed the relationship.

Calvin's eyes went wide. "Leave Macy out of this. She don't know nothing, King. She don't—"

"You tried to rob me. Do you think I trust you to tell me the truth? Dave, go get Macy," Romelo said. Dave backed away, looking horrified. The King didn't kill women and girls.

"King, you sure?" he asked, his voice low. Romelo turned to him, scowling.

"Your man thinks he can play with me, and I say let's play. Go get her."

"King, please. Macy didn't do it. I played her, she wasn't in on it. I swear," Calvin yelled. Truck swung the bat and connected with his dick. Calvin screamed.

"Don't talk now, bitch," Truck spat, "We gave you a chance."

"Dave, take care of your problem so I can go home," Romelo said, his voice tired. Dave looked around the room, at Calvin moaning through the pain; at the man beside him bleeding out in real time, at Truck and Easy and the weapons in their hands. Dave sighed, and pulled his gun, walking up to Calvin. Three shots to the chest and he was gone. Dave stepped back, his hand shaking. Easy took the gun from him, putting it in his pocket. Romelo nodded, keenly aware of Dave's reluctance, and his reaction.

"Clean-up's on the way, Boss," Teddy said, from the dark corner where he'd been watching. Romelo put his gun away, making a mental note to have Sadie prep a new one for Dave. Truck handed him a plastic bag with the weapons and phones they'd taken from their three wannabe thieves. He'd have Sadie wipe them clean and properly dispose of them.

"Dave, stay with Truck and Easy until cleanup comes. I'll reach out tomorrow after I talk to Keys," Romelo said. Everyone nodded and Romelo left.

In the back of the car, he leaned back and closed his eyes. His head pain was sharper now, without the adrenaline to push it away. He needed his girls. And he needed to sleep.

Bianca

Bianca whimpered, her thighs shaking as they tightened around Romelo's head. His long tongue swirled around her clit and over the wet folds of her pussy. She was moving her hips to the rhythm his mouth set, twerking on his face, and nothing had ever felt so good. Bianca moaned as lips pulled her nipples. Sadie was facing her, riding Romelo's dick, leaning forward to brace herself on his chest and lick at Bianca's breasts.

"Yes, baby. Don't stop," she cried. Romelo held her thighs and sucked her clit into his mouth with firm pressure. Bianca fell apart, leaking on his face, yelling his name.

"Fuck, fuck, fuck," Sadie moaned, moving up and down on their man's long, hard, dick. Bianca was overwhelmed, pleasure and lust filling her up, soft noises pushing from her throat. She hadn't danced in two days, but her body had been worked over, bent and twisted all the same. She told herself today she'd go to her place and rest; she'd stretch and dance. But Romelo used the magic of his mouth, hands, and dick to keep her in his sights and Bianca had no willpower when the King called her name.

Since the shooting at the club, Romelo had been in a cycle of dealing with Sparkle City being temporarily shut down, handling street business, and making love to her and Sadie like he was afraid of them disappearing. He needed them within arm's reach as often as possible, on top and underneath him as much as they could handle. Bianca knew it was his way of working through his fear of losing them. She was only too willing to be his comfort, to let him be hers, to get lost in him.

"Ro, babyyyyyy. Fuck!" she yelled, releasing over his mouth, yet again. Romelo licked her clean, slurping her wetness, moaning from Sadie moving on top of him. Bianca finally managed to fall off his face and collapse on the bed.

"Come inside me, King. *Dame tus bebes* (Give me your babies)," Sadie moaned, her skin flushed and her body shaking. She fell onto Romelo's chest, and he held her in place, pumping into her until he came, hard.

"Fuck!" he yelled. The three of them lay there, catching their breath. Sadie was the first to find the strength to get up and head to the shower. Bianca kissed Romelo's juicy lips and followed her. She was pretty sure he'd be asleep by the time they came out. Bianca covered her hair with a shower cap and walked into the giant shower. The wall jets covered her and Sadie in a hot, relaxing, spray of water. Sadie soaped a loofah and started washing Bianca, leaning up to kiss her lips. Bianca giggled, wrapped her tongue around Sadie's and grabbed for her softness. She loved that her girlfriend had so much to hold onto.

"Behave, so I can clean you up," Sadie ordered and finished washing her. Once Bianca returned the favor and they were both clean, Bianca sat on the bench and tugged Sadie over. She lifted Sadie's legs and placed her foot beside her on the bench before parting Sadie's pussy lips with her fingers and rubbing her clit while she licked her nipples. Sadie moved her hips, whimpering.

"Beeeeee," she cried, taking her pleasure, reaching for paradise. Bianca sped up her hand, dipping two fingers inside, sliding over the swollen nub of desire with her thumb until Sadie came on a breathless sigh. Then she started again, finger fucking her girlfriend and thumbing her clit while she filled her mouth with Sadie's breasts. Sadie's noises turned her on, made her wet. Bianca's sore pussy couldn't handle anymore, but fucking Sadie had her on the verge of coming too. Sadie yelled her name, moving her ample hips back and forth, her sweet, sticky, release coating Bianca's fingers. Bianca felt her pussy clench and then she came, whimpering softly as she stuck her fingers in her mouth, tasting Sadie's honey.

"You are beautiful when you come for me," she said. Sadie kissed her mouth over and over, whispering her love. The two of them washed themselves once more before finally getting out of the shower.

As expected, Romelo was asleep, which gave Bianca time to get dressed and slip away. She promised Sadie she'd be back for dinner and Teddy followed her to her apartment. Once there, she redressed in a leotard and tights and headed into the private principal dancer studio, which was thankfully empty.

After a good stretch, Bianca got into a groove, dancing freestyle, mixing her classical training with her natural born rhythm and contemporary movements. An hour of dancing after a morning of making love and Bianca was wrecked. She headed back through the school to her place, took the fastest shower known to man and fell into her bed, sleep coming quickly.

Bianca woke to the smell of food. She sat up in bed, disoriented at first. Then she noticed she'd been placed under the blankets and arranged more comfortably on her pillows, and there was a bonnet on her hair. Her sweaty dance clothes had disappeared from where she'd left them in the middle of the floor, and there was an aromatherapy candle burning. Bianca got out of bed, confused. She had a pretty good idea who had come to take care of her, but how long had she slept? She opened her bedroom door and walked the short hallway.

Sadie and Romelo were in the kitchen, laughing and talking at the stove. They looked up when they noticed her, smiling.

"What's going on?" Bianca asked, her voice still soft with sleep.

Romelo grinned. "You slept through lunch and when we called to remind you about dinner, you didn't answer."

"We came to make sure you were alright and realized we tired you out," Sadie jumped in, "We needed to make sure you ate so we decided to do dinner here."

"Thank you," Bianca said, smiling big. She went further into the kitchen, leaning over to inspect the pots.

"You two sit down," Romelo instructed, "I'm bringing the food to you. Go cuddle on the couch or something." The two women listened and grabbed hands, hurrying to the sofa. Bianca chose a movie, but she ended up much more preoccupied with Sadie's kisses, and her hands.

Shortly after, Romelo walked in with plates. He set the plates down and went away, coming back with two glasses of wine. Then, he went to get the food.

"Chicken stir fry over jasmine rice for my girls," he announced, setting a big platter down with a serving spoon inside. He went back to the kitchen, and Bianca started making plates, realizing she was ravenous. Romelo came back for the final time with napkins, utensils, hoisin sauce, and a beer for himself. He sat on the floor and grabbed his plate. Sadie said a short prayer, and then there was only the sound of eating. Bianca tucked into her food, feeling so blessed. Her lovers took care of her like no one ever had. Being able to dance out her dreams and come home to them was everything.

"Bee, I want to ask you to do something for me," Romelo said, swallowing his food. Bianca looked into his eyes. There wasn't much she'd say no to if Romelo was asking.

"Okay, baby. Ask me to do what?"

"I want you to let Sadie teach you how to shoot, and give you a gun," he said, putting his plate down and facing her fully. Bianca immediately wanted to protest. Romelo had begged her to practice with him at his range behind the house. He wanted to teach her the basics, so she'd know what to do if she was threatened. But Bianca felt sick every time she thought of it. She knew who her man was, and what he did, but having her life reach the level of violence where she needed to use a gun was too much. She was too afraid then, and she was too afraid now. She started shaking her head.

"Ro, I—"

"Baby, please," he begged, "You know it's something I've wanted since we met. And in the past, when you said you were too afraid, I didn't push you. But after what happened at the club, I... I need to know you two have all the options available to you. I will give my life and every resource I have to protect you, but I can't be with you all the time. Please, let Sadie show you how to protect yourself."

"Romelo, I would do anything for you," Bianca whispered, "But this is... I don't know if I can handle this. You know what happened to me."

"What happened?" Sadie asked. Bianca felt tears coming to her eyes.

"Gun violence is how Bee lost her mother," Romelo said lowly, "It's how she became an orphan."

"A senseless act. A stupid convenience store robbery took my mother, who was only trying to make it home with milk for me. I... I barely remember anything from when she died, but I remember being 16 and finally asking my parents if they knew what happened to her. I remember reading the police report. I've never wanted anything to do with guns since."

"Bee, why didn't you ever tell me?" Sadie demanded. Bianca shrugged.

"Because I never had to. Unlike Romelo, your love of guns was something you were happy to keep me far away from. You see them as a hobby, and you never questioned why I wasn't into them. You simply saw it as a way we differed in our upbringing. Ro, on the other hand, sees them as necessary evil in his life, as a way to be prepared—and he can't have the people he loves out in the world unprepared, so he kept pressing the issue. I finally had to tell him why I was so afraid."

"Fear is natural, Bee. As many guns as I've fired, I'm still not completely calm holding one. But I think you'd benefit from facing the fear, and I think Sadie is the person who should help you tackle it. You two love and understand each other, and Sadie is patient and even more knowledgeable than me. If anyone can help you conquer this, it's her," Romelo said, pointing at their girlfriend.

Sadie took her hand. "Oh love, I wish you'd told me. But I understand you not wanting to relive the hurt. I can help you, if you let me. And this would be a last resort, a skill you acquire to use *if* you ever need it. Not a lifestyle. Okay, babe? Let me help you, because I need you protected too."

Bianca was quiet. Her lovers' words echoed in her mind, making her think. If Romelo and Sadie were in this life, and she was determined to be in it with them, she had to readjust. Her hands shook a little after Sadie let go. Could she do this? Bianca reached for the necklace Romelo returned to her, the necklace she never took off anymore for any reason. The heart charm at the end warmed in her fingers and she thought of her mother.

"Okay," Bianca whispered, "I'll try. I'll let you show me how to shoot. But I don't want my own gun. I'm not ready for that yet."

"Then we'll start tomorrow," Sadie said, bringing her close. They kissed lingeringly, and Bianca picked up her plate again. Romelo winked at her mouthing, *I'm proud of you*, and Bianca felt warm. She was actually a little proud of herself.

Seven

L abor Day
 Bianca

Trevino still wasn't the kind of person who liked people in his home, but here they all were again, having another family cookout. She, Romelo, and Sadie arrived just in time for Sadie to rest herself with Nasima and Keona, in comfy chairs underneath an umbrella for shade. The two of them were beautifully pregnant, glowing and growing, nurturing the babies everyone couldn't wait to meet. Easy and EJ tossed a ball back and forth at the other end of the yard while Trevino worked the grill and Bashir brought things from inside the house.

"You sit down too," Romelo ordered, pressing a cup into her hand and kissing her forehead before going to help his cousin. Bianca relaxed, smiling. He was taking such good care of her and Sadie. The school's second show had closed; Bianca was a principal dancer with a solo in the second act, plus as per her job description, she worked on the choreography and formations. The night before, was the finale of two weeks of nightly performances.

"Bee, you were so great last night," Nasima gushed. The entire family, Truck and Easy included, had come to the final performance, "You move so gracefully. I always wanted to do ballet."

"We have adult beginner classes, Nas. I don't teach them, but they're really good. You can come for exercise while you're pregnant, and after the baby's born, keep it going," Bianca encouraged.

Nasima shook her head. "I'm too fat for ballet, aren't I?"

"Hell no," Bianca refuted, "I will admit the professional ballet world can be very thin-centered. But if you're doing it for fun, and because you love to dance, we have modifications that can make it work for any size. And with enough practice, you can move like me."

"Really?" Nasima said, her eyes wide. Bianca nodded.

"Absolutely. I used to make Sadie practice with me all the time."

"I only did it because I knew I'd get to twist you up afterwards," Sadie admitted. The ladies broke into laughter. They sipped their drinks and relaxed while the men brought everything together. Soon, others were trickling in: MomMom, Easy's grandmother, plus a couple of her bridge-playing friends; Linc and Bunky, the two guys who ran Bashir's gym; Malice and Keys, with their girlfriends; of course, Scratch and Teddy, plus Bashir's friend Markeese, and Finley, who worked for the organization in a way Bianca wasn't clear on. If she didn't know better, she'd swear he and Markeese were on a date. They arrived together, Markeese stuck to Finley like he didn't want to lose him, and Finley was so attentive, making sure Markeese was eating, drinking, and having fun. She smiled. Her own connection made her appreciate all romantic things.

Music and food started flowing, and Bianca was having the time of her life. She felt so settled, so calm. She was finally home. Her love was flourishing, and she didn't want for anything. Her dancing was better than ever, and she was even being brave despite her reservations and learning to shoot.

Romelo whispered to Truck as they stood at the grill together; Bianca knew they were all worried about someone named Dave being absent today. She hoped it would all turn out okay. But she wasn't worried about drama at the cookout. Nobody who loved their life would play with Truck like that. Romelo caught her eye, winking and blowing her a kiss.

"Ladies," Bashir said, walking over with a huge tray of food, "I got some salmon and veggies for the ballerina, barbecue chicken and macaroni salad for Keona the Mama, sausage and peppers and potato salad for Lil Baby, and ribs and mac and cheese for Sadie the Shooter."

The women laughed at his descriptions while taking their plates. Bianca dug into her food, loving the smokey flavor of the grilled corn, peppers, zucchini, and yellow squash.

"These men of ours got us so spoiled," Keona said, mouth full, "All Elliott wants me to do is sit and eat. He told me after I have this baby he's getting us a nanny. MomMom was very offended, but I was amazed. He'll really do anything to make me happy."

"Speaking of spoiled, Romelo's trying to figure out if he has enough room for a stable behind his house so Sadie can bring her horses here," Bianca said.

"You have horses?" Keona asked.

Sadie nodded. "Two. My daddy taught me two things he said everyone should know: how to ride and shoot. He said the rest was on my mama." The women laughed.

"Horses sound fun. But there's a gun range already back there. Won't the shooting spook them?" Nasima asked.

Sadie pouted. "Probably, which is why he's making me choose."

The women laughed again and went back to eating.

The afternoon turned into evening, and the party continued. Markeese cut loose and got very tipsy, which they found out was a celebration of him escaping an abusive relationship, and Finley took such good care of him. They left together, and Bashir made a comment about Markeese being "safe for once." Bianca smiled; safety was everything. She looked at Sadie. She was in Romelo's lap while he whispered in her ear and rubbed her thighs. Sadie giggled, then looked up, catching her gaze. She waved her over and Bianca went, happy she was safe now too.

Romelo

Romelo woke up to two tongues on his hardening dick and thought surely, he'd died and gone to heaven. His fine ass women licked and caressed him, taking their satisfaction from him. He opened his eyes and shifted slightly, grinning down at them. A moment later, one of his balls was in Sadie's mouth and Bianca had swallowed his dick.

"Shit!" Romelo yelled, the sensations making him feel weak. Pleasure hummed throughout his entire body. Bianca suctioned him perfectly, letting him touch the back of her throat. Sadie licked lovingly as she held his balls in her mouth, using her hand to caress his sensitive areas. Romelo moaned loudly, feeling like the luckiest nigga alive. The King was waking up to head.

"You taste so good, baby," Bee whispered, swallowing him again. Sadie mumbled in agreement, her mouth busy. Romelo raised his hips, feeding himself to them, balling the sheets in his fist. His head spun, the excitement and ecstasy making him close his eyes. But he forced them open again, wanting to see his girls love him with their mouths.

"My turn, Bee," Sadie pouted, sitting up. Bianca giggled and they switched places, Sadie sliding his entire dick into her mouth while Bianca played with his balls.

"Oh my—fuck—shit!" Romelo could barely catch his breath, could barely hang on. He was getting closer with every slurp, every lick, every kiss.

"I'm gonna—I gotta—" he tried to speak, but the suction on his dick and balls were stealing his words.

"It's okay, baby," Sadie whispered, "*Déjalo ir. Danos todo* (Let go. Give us everything)."

Romelo shouted, releasing in thick spurts and Sadie swallowed without even blinking. She moved and Bianca slapped his dick against her tongue, coaxing the last of his release into her mouth. Romelo lay there, his mind blown. He'd never felt anything so sexy and consuming in his life. Bianca and Sadie each moved up to his side and lay against him.

"Good morning to you too," he pushed out, still trying to breathe. His two women laughed and snuggled closer.

Later, King, Truck, and Easy were on the early morning count as usual, discussing the mounting evidence they had labeling Dave a traitor. Romelo was still pissed off it had come to this. He trusted Dave. He and Malice were the same age as Truck and Easy, and he'd brought them all in together. They'd been essential to the takeover that brought him his first set of blocks.

"Okay, what all do we have so far?" Romelo asked.

Easy separated a stack of money. "First, one of his bags was light. My guess is it was an initial deposit to whoever is helping him orchestrate this shit."

"Plus, stealing from you is a loyalty test. I'm sure he passed," Truck added.

Romelo nodded. "Him and Calvin set Jamir up as a patsy and start moving corner boys around."

"I think it was about infiltration," Easy said, "I bet he put some snitches in the rotation and started switching corners to throw us off. Doing pick-ups and re-ups, I'm the only one who might know everybody. And we let him, and Malice handle their own recruitment."

"Are they planning a mutiny or something? Trying to take us over from the inside?"

"Sounds like it," Romelo answered his cousin, "I think he's been trying to bring in people loyal to him, not us. They're probably like our two thieves. Niggas who used to be with the Wolf and need a new hustle."

"Maybe next time you'll listen to me when I say kill everybody," Truck said with a smirk.

Romelo's cell phone rang. He answered and put it on speaker. "Keys, what's up?"

"Did some digging on Calvin. Turns out, he was in deep with Dave and lost his nerve at the last minute. The planned robbery at Sparkle City was supposed to happen at a handful of your other legit spots too. Him and Dave wanted you distracted so they could make their own moves. Still don't know who their other partner is though. I'll keep looking."

"Thanks, Keys," Romelo replied and hung up, making a mental note to send him a bonus.

A knock sounded at the door and Teddy stuck his head in. "Malice needs to see you, King."

"Send him in," Romelo said. Teddy nodded and a second later, Malik "Malice," Johnson walked in. He was 34, the same age as Truck and Easy, and ran the corners on the West Side, while Dave was in charge on the east. He was loyal, intelligent, and calculating.

"Sup, Malice. What's good?"

"I got some information you need. It's connected to whatever Dave has been doing."

"What is it?" Trevino said, sitting up straight. Malice looked around the room, his eyes regretful but resolute.

"He got a new young nigga on his team, named Marco or some shit—"

"The kid whose girlfriend was breaking the phones because he was cheating," Romelo jumped in. Malice's eyes widened, like he was surprised Romelo knew the situation.

He nodded. "Yeah, that's the one. He's been spending a lot of time with a girl who lives on my side."

"So, the kid's stupid, but it doesn't sound major," Easy said, "Who's the girl?"

"It's not about the girl; it's about her people. She's Chloe Burns," Malice announced, "Her uncle is a public defender named Rick Burns."

"I know his name from somewhere," Truck said, rubbing his chin thoughtfully, "Keep talking. It'll come to me."

"He's one of those tough-on-crime niggas who's actually a criminal himself. Anyway, it turns out Marco knows Chloe because he got in some trouble years ago, and Rick Burns was the PD who pleaded him out, got him off with probation."

"It was about infiltration then. Burns had Dave put Marco on," Romelo finished, his eyes narrowing, "Where the fuck is Dave?"

"I don't know. But I told him last week Marco was spending too much time on my side for somebody who was supposed to be working for *him*. He told me he'd take care of it, but he hasn't. When I remembered who Chloe was connected to, I figured Burns might be the third person you were looking for."

"You're probably right. Malice, I need you to put eyes on Rick Burns and keep them there. I mean, I don't want him to take a shit without me knowing. Easy, I need you to hit the street on Dave's side and see what the other workers are saying. If Rick Burns is the opps, it makes sense he'd try to set up the house across from the trap," Romelo started giving orders, getting angrier by the second.

"But what's Burns' endgame? Taking the East side?" Easy said, anger on his face.

"A territory dispute has a ripple effect. Keeps us preoccupied and more exposed, more hands on—like when we first started taking blocks. Maybe he was planning to touch one of us. But I also think he's hoping to weaken us by setting off infighting and disloyalty," Truck said.

"You're right," Romelo agreed, "And it's forcing us back to our roots. We've been branching out, moving into other shit because we had a lock on the streets. If shit is shaky on our home base, in the place that made us, it's time to pull back. Put our foot back on everybody's neck."

"You need anything else from me, King?" Malice asked.

Romelo nodded his head. "One more thing: send a couple of our young niggas who like to tear shit up to get Marco and Chloe. Hold them for a minute. Trev, you and I are gonna run up on Dave," Romelo finished. Malice left the room, and the other three started stacking money and putting it in the safe. The count would have to wait.

Two Days Later

Romelo walked into the back entrance of the laundromat and veered right. He knocked the wall on the left side and a panel opened to a stairway.

"Scratch, watch the cameras. Teddy, you're with me," Romelo went down the stairs as the panel closed behind him and Teddy. When he got to the bottom, he went to the iron door and punched his code into the keypad. He and Teddy entered the main area. Truck and Easy stood off to the side, talking quietly. In the center of the room, both Marco and Dave were tied to chairs, their faces bruised and bleeding. Someone was whimpering in the shadowy corner, but Romelo wasn't concerned with them. Teddy walked off in the direction of the whimper and a few moments later it was quiet.

"Why it smell like piss in here?" Romelo sneered, wrinkling his nose.

Trevino rolled his eyes. "Apparently, Marco has a bladder problem. Can't even take a punch, lil bitch ass."

"Let's get this shit over with, then. What you been telling your side bitch and her uncle about my operation, Marco?"

"Chloe is just a fri—nothing, King. I swear, I ain't tell them nothing!" Marco cried. Romelo sighed.

"I heard you been spending a lot of time with Chloe. Dapping up her cop uncle, dropping bags at the mall and shit. What you say when she asked you where all the money came from?"

"All I said was you hooked me up, man! And I was gonna get my own corner soon! But no specifics, King. I promise," Marco yelled.

"That's specific enough for me. You think I don't know who sent you here? Plus, you said you ain't tell her nothing and you obviously told her something. I don't like liars, Marco," Romelo said.

"Come on, King. I wanted to take care of my family, man. I got a girl! I got a kid!"

"Bitch, please. You don't give a fuck about your family for real, or you would have thought this through. But don't worry, I'll make sure your kid's new daddy is a real nigga," Romelo laughed, gesturing to Easy. Easy walked over with a baseball bat and swung, smashing it against Marco's knee. He screamed and then whimpered as he passed out from the pain.

"Man, this shit ain't even fun. Did he pass out?" Easy said, dropping the bat in disgust. Trevino doubled over with laughter. Romelo chuckled and walked over to Dave.

"David," he said calmly, holding out his hand behind him. His cousin put a gun into it, "My sources tell me Rick Burns goes back a ways with our friend Marco here. He defended him on some petty theft charges, pleaded him out, and then sent him to you when he got off probation. Now, since you brought Marco in, and I'm assuming you did the necessary checks before you did so, you're either working with Rick or fucking stupid. Care to tell me which one it is?"

"I didn't know, King. It's a lot of corners, and I'm pushing a lot of weight. His money never came up short, so I thought he was good," Dave mumbled. Romelo shook his head, took aim and shot into Dave's kneecap. The man screamed in pain.

"I didn't ask you what you thought. I asked you if you checked his story when he told you who referred him for the work. I'm asking if you knew he'd been cycled through the public defender's office and ended up fucking the niece of said public defender."

"He said he wanted to feed his family, get his girl out the hood. I believed him," Dave said, his chest heaving as he struggled to speak.

"But you didn't handle the shit with the phones," Easy jumped in, "When you missed it, I told you to tighten up. Ain't no way you didn't know who he was working for. Plus, you reported seeing somebody at the house across from the trap when we know nobody was living there. A house owned by Rick Burns' mother."

"Things have been slipping on the East side for a while, Dave. And we kept giving you chance after chance to handle your shit. But you never did. You continued to do dirt, and took Calvin's life because he didn't want to do it with you anymore." Truck said, stepping closer. He didn't have a gun, but he didn't need one. Trevino "Truck" Davis took his family seriously and the penalty for playing in Romelo's face was pain, and death. Dave's eyes widened and he swallowed, hard. Romelo knew he'd been hoping for a quick death, but with Truck here, there was no hope.

"Sounds like you're lying to us, David. Tell you what—tell me what Burns promised you, and I'll call Truck off and make this quick and painless," Romelo said. Dave refused to answer, and like Calvin, he had to respect it. Man's gotta have a code. He whistled and Malice and Teddy appeared from the shadows with public defender Rick Burns and his niece Chloe. Chloe was hysterical, sobbing and nearly hyperventilating. Dave hung his head.

Rick Burns looked shell shocked. "Look, King—spare my niece, man. She's young—"

"She's old enough to suck and fuck niggas for information and hand it off to you," Romelo said angrily, going over to Rick and hitting him across the face with the gun, "Her mama know you been pimping her like this?"

He turned to Chloe. "Your mama know you opening your legs for corner boys so your uncle can plead them out and turn them into snitches?" Chloe shook her head, still sobbing, her entire body shaking. Romelo sighed. He hated this. But everyone had to learn their lesson.

"We don't kill young girls, King. You said women and children were untouchable," Dave begged, his fear finally showing. Romelo scowled.

"Ain't nobody gonna kill her," he said, "But she is going to watch you, her uncle, and her boyfriend die so she knows I'm a serious man who doesn't like when people try to sabotage me. Then I'm going to put someone on *her* people, so she knows I can get to her any time I want. Maybe with the right influence, and the threat of having her entire family wiped from the face of the fucking Earth, Chloe can make something of herself one day, who knows?"

"And she's better off without her uncle anyway," Trevino said, wrapping his hands like he was preparing for a boxing match, "Now, I remember where I know you from, Counselor. Bashir told me how you abused Markeese, how you talked down to him, and beat him. And didn't I see you trying to hem him up in the hardware store? Looks like karma could be catching up with you."

"You're good, Rome. We got this," Easy said. Romelo nodded and turned to leave, Teddy following. He'd have to figure out who to handle Dave's corners, and why his trusted lieutenant would betray him after all these years, but they were problems for tomorrow. He left the room and went back up the stairs, tapping on the left wall so the panel would open. He exited and headed out the back door, with Teddy, and now Scratch, on his heels. They got into the car and sped away. Romelo sat back against the seat, sighing deeply.

"Truck's gonna need clean up," he said quietly, and closed his eyes for the ride home.

By the time the car dropped him off, Romelo's head was on fire, and he could barely see straight. He tried to get up to his bed without seeing either of his girls—he hadn't eaten or hydrated enough today, and he knew they'd be on his ass about it. He got to the bedroom without incident and got undressed. Romelo climbed into bed and closed his eyes. He wished he'd remembered a cool rag to put across his forehead.

"I cannot believe you tried to sneak by without telling us you were hurting," Bianca said in an annoyed whisper. She entered the bedroom with Sadie behind her.

"I didn't want you to worry. I'll be fine in a couple of hours," Romelo insisted.

"We're worried anyway. Baby, did you eat today?" Sadie said.

"Naw, but we had a lot of business to handle today, and none of it was good."

"We're so sorry, love," Bianca said, climbing up beside him. Sadie got in on the other side and put a cool towel on his neck while Bianca rubbed his temples. The relief took a few minutes, but it eventually came. Romelo drifted off to sleep, surrounded by the faint smell of lavender.

When he woke up, he was alone again, but the table in the sitting area had a stack of plates, wine and bottled water, which meant his women had most likely gone to get food. Romelo picked up his phone. He had a slew of unread texts, from Truck and Easy saying everything was taken care of; from Keys and Malice giving him updates; from his pharmacy about his migraine medication, and one from an unknown number with seven words: *Call me. We need to talk business.*

Romelo dialed the number, recognizing the area code, and knowing it could only be one person.

"Kamal? When did you get out?"

Sadie

Days and weeks passed since Bee rejoined their home, and the next thing Sadie knew, they were almost fully autumn. Nas and Key were finally showing, Bee was becoming a great shooter under her tutelage and her King was still the King. There'd been some hiccups for sure, but everything seemed to be falling into place the way it was intended. Except for one thing.

"Romelo, I want to keep the gun range. I don't want the stable anymore," Sadie conceded, sitting on his lap and eating pasta. Bianca didn't do a lot of cooking, but she made the best Bolognese sauce in the world. It started with a sofrito, slow-cooked with veal and pork, tomatoes and a bunch of red wine. Sadie was having the time of her life with her bowl of food.

"We could always bring the horses here anyway, board them locally," he said, rubbing her thighs and watching TV. They were in the den, and Bee was in Romelo's office on a video call with her friends from the dance troupe.

Sadie sighed. "Maybe."

"I'll call someone to see if there's a place nearby, baby," Romelo said, focused on women's basketball. Sadie twirled more pasta on her fork. This was probably her favorite thing about Romelo. He was very solution focused.

"Really? That easily?"

"I have told you a million times I will do anything to make you happy. Sometimes, I think you ask me for shit just to make me prove it to you. But yes, I'll do it, Shug," Romelo replied, kissing her neck. Sadie giggled. She did love being Romelo's spoiled Shug, even when he was annoyed, she was demanding too much attention.

"Knowing you'll do anything for my happiness makes me feel a whole lot more confident about having this baby," Sadie said nonchalantly, stuffing her mouth. Romelo nodded absently, then turned to her as her words finally registered.

"What did you say?"

"Why? What do you think I said?" Sadie laughed.

"I think she said she's having a baby," Bianca said from the doorway. Romelo stared at her, surprise and happiness coming over his face. He took the bowl from her hands and hugged her so tightly.

"Seriously, Shug? You not playing with me, are you?"

"I'd never play about this, Ro," Sadie grinned. Romelo smiled so wide, her heart fluttered. He was really her Prince Charming, her dark knight, the one who made the world spin faster. *He's going to be an amazing father*, she thought. Then she looked up at her dancer girl. The one who kept her tethered, so she didn't float away. Bianca completed her heart, completed their family. Sadie had no worries about being a mother, not with these two by her side. And she'd never worry about being too much or not enough, ever again.

"Thank you. I love you, I love you so much," Romelo said, kissing her face. Sadie smiled. She'd found out earlier in the day but wanted to wait until they were all together to share the news.

"You're our miracle, Shug," he continued. Sadie kissed his lips as tears came to her eyes. Bianca sat beside them, wrapping her arms around the back of Sadie as Romelo held tight to her front.

"We're going to be parents," Bianca said. Sadie nodded. It was her perfect dream.

"I wouldn't have wanted to do this without you, Bee," she whispered, "Thank you for coming home."

"Thank you two for leaving the light on," Bianca whispered back.

Epilogue

<h2>An Invitation</h2>

Nine Months Later

Romelo

Teddy pulled up in front of a four-story brownstone. It was reminiscent of the New York City style, though there were no houses on either side, and they were hours north of New York City. Scratch and Teddy got out of the front seat and opened the back doors, letting Romelo, Bianca, and Sadie out of the car. Behind him, Trevino was helping Nasima from the car with Bashir getting out after them. The kids, Trevino's son and Romelo's daughter, were back at home with Easy and Keona and their kids. The invitation was for Romelo, his second-in-command, and their partners. Before they could climb the stairs, the heavy door opened, and a dark-skinned man with his long hair in a bun stood at the top.

"My name is Paxton Montana," he said, his voice strong, but kind, "We've been expecting you." He gestured to them and Romelo took Bianca and Sadie's hands and climbed the stairs into the house, Truck, Nasima, and Bashir bringing up the rear. The front entryway was flanked by vining plants whose branches crept up the wall and wrapped around and anchored with shiny marble floors. The group followed Paxton through a great room, past an opulent dining room, and finally into an atrium. Sadie and Bianca gasped at the tall ceilings, and the glass wall bringing natural light into the room. It was filled with plants of all kinds, some flowering, some not, and there was soft music playing through a sound system.

"We can make the initial introductions here, and then Kamal and King Davis will separate to have their meeting while the rest of us get to know each other," Paxton said.

As soon as he stopped speaking, a door opened on the other side of the room. The first one to walk in was a woman with short, red, curly hair, styled in a fauxhawk. She was fat—her shape was like Nas and Sadie's—and gorgeous with her enormous eyes and full mouth. One look at her though, and Romelo knew she was a dangerous woman. Behind her was another man, tall and medium brown, with eyes so dark and menacing a lesser man than Romelo would have backed away. The last person to enter was the man he'd come to see. Kamal Mason. Heir to the Commission.

"King Davis," Kamal said, walking toward him with a smirk. The two men exchanged a handshake and a hug.

"Mal. Good to see you on this side of the bars, man."

"It took fucking long enough. Introduce me to your people. If I have my way, we're gonna spend a good amount of time together," Kamal said. Romelo chuckled. He and Kamal went back years. Kamal was the heir to a multi-family alliance called The Commission, a vast criminal enterprise with reach all over this side of the country. Twelve years before, The Commission was targeted, and every family head was killed. Kamal was blamed and thrown into prison. Now out on a technicality, he was rebuilding what he'd lost. Coming for his crown. And grinding everyone who accused him into dust.

When Romelo got the call, he was pretty sure he knew why Kamal wanted to see him and he was planning to say yes. He had a feeling it was exactly what his family needed. He gestured to the two amazing women holding his hands.

"I'm Romelo Davis. Most people call me King. These are my loves, Bianca Bellamy and Sadie Wells. You know my cousin, Trevino, or Truck. These are his two partners, Nasima Jones and

Bashir Rosewood." After he finished, the women waved while Truck and Bash gave Kamal the head nod.

Kamal's mouth lifted in an almost smile. "It's a pleasure to meet y'all. I'm Kamal Mason. These are my partners, Asani Lucas-Mason, Pax Montana, and Ethan Turner."

"Truck Davis?" Ethan stepped forward, an impressed look on his face, "*Thee* Truck Davis?"

Truck laughed. "'Sup, man. Aye yo, whatever you heard about me, don't believe it."

"Yeah, don't believe it," Nasima spoke up, "Because whatever you heard, the truth is worse."

Everyone laughed after her statement.

Kamal shook his head. "We're gonna have some food brought in. Y'all get comfortable; make yourselves at home. King and I will be back soon. Ro, let's go to my office." Kamal led the way and Romelo followed. They stepped into a huge office, with three desks, oak shelving lined with books, and big windows. Kamal sat behind the biggest desk and Romelo sat in the chair in front of it.

"I'm glad you came, man. It took longer than I thought to get things together."

"I understand," Romelo said, "You were away a long time."

"For some shit I didn't do. Pax and E kept me sane while I was down. That's why I didn't move without them," Kamal said.

Romelo nodded. "Completely understandable. When did you get a wife though?"

Kamal smiled fully now, his expression devious. "She's, *our* wife. And technically, we stole her."

Romelo laughed loudly, shaking his head. Same old Kamal. "Some things never change, my nigga. You always did hate asking permission. But she's clearly no shrinking violet. I'm surprised she didn't kill you."

"She tried," Kamal shrugged, "then she realized she loved me."

"Sounds like your destiny. Either way, I'm happy for you."

"Thanks, man. I'm happy for you too. All grown up, with two beautiful women, got niggas calling you King and praising your product. You're in the weapons business now too, right?"

"Yeah, I am. It's been mostly a side venture. I haven't devoted the proper time to it. I don't think I would have held on this long if Sadie didn't love guns so much," Romelo admitted.

"The short one? Yeah, she looks like she'd shoot you," Kamal laughed, "Tell you what. What if I take the weapons venture off your hands, and expand your drug territories? You can do what you're good at, under our umbrella. I already know how good you are, and how tight a ship you run. Your organization is exactly the presence I need. These people need to see power. And a man as knowledgeable, focused, and settled in himself as you are is power personified. Think about it. Protection. Incentives. Family. Become a part of what I'm rebuilding. You know what kind of reach the Barrett Brothers had. You'd take their place at the table."

Romelo smiled. It was a great opportunity. Of course, there'd be more work, but expansion was never a bad thing. And now that he'd weeded out the snakes, he and his most loyal could get what was theirs, with the kind of protection they never had before. The Mason name still rung bells and this move would take Romelo's power and product even further.

"Sounds like a plan, man. Let's do it," he said. Kamal held out his hand. Romelo shook it.

"This is the start of something greater. We'll iron out the details after we eat with our families. But for now, welcome to The Commission, King Davis."

Acknowledgements

Jaleesa- Always. In all ways. Thank you for everything.
Kimmie- Who always calls when I summon you, lol.
Nicole Falls- You teach me how to keep going.
Shon- So inspirational.
The Chary Assist- You saved me. Thank you.
My babies from the Discord, all my bookish baddies, and the people who laugh at my jokes

Gran, I miss you every day.

About the Author

Shameka Erby is a writer from Philadelphia currently living in Baltimore. Her love affair with romance novels started early, and she loves writing sweet and sexy love stories. Now the author of four short story collections and twelve romantic novels, Shameka's joy is in writing gentle, emotional, passionately heated stories of Black love starring plus sized and queer characters. She also publishes a newsletter, Just A Girl and Her Laptop.

Books By Shameka S. Erby

The McNeals
The Driver's Seat
Find My Way Back
The Officer and the Butterfly
The Greatest Risk

The Royals
Hooked on Your Love
Until You Come Back To Me
All I Need
Don't Play That Song
The Going Away Present: A Mal and Luchi Short
Love Notes: Sexy Holiday Stories

Coming Home: The Elements Series
The Air Between Us
Her Solid Ground
The Pick-Up

Luna Lake
All I Want For Christmas Is Two
Hearts Afire

Short Story Collections
Accessories of Love
Heartbreak Alley
Blood Ties